Holidays Can Be Murder
A Charlie Parker Christmas Mystery

Connie Shelton

Holidays Can Be Murder
Published by Secret Staircase Books, an imprint of
Columbine Publishing Group
PO Box 416, Angel Fire, NM 87710

Printed and bound in the United States of America
ISBN 1449519733
ISBN-13 978-1449519735

Book layout and design by Secret Staircase Books
Cover image © Darren Fisher
Cover silhouettes © Majivecka

First publication of "Holidays Can Be Murder" appeared in the anthology *How
Still We See Thee Lie*, 2002, Worldwide Mystery. All rights reverted to the author.

First publication in book format, December 2009
First e-book edition: December 2009

Holidays Can Be Murder

A Charlie Parker Christmas Mystery

Connie Shelton

Author's Note

I hope you enjoy this holiday mystery with Charlie and Drake, their pets and family. This novella was originally published in book club format by Worldwide Mystery under the guidance of my editor and friend, Feroze Mohammad. It was his suggestion that I write a Christmas mystery and I had a wonderful time doing it. Keep in mind that it was written in 2002, which places it between the other titles in my series, *Honeymoons Can Be Murder* and *Reunions Can Be Murder.* Still, the holiday traditions in Albuquerque remain much the same as I remember them from my early years, with the addition of a few fictional ones I've created for purposes of this story. Enjoy!

Chapter 1

The holidays bring out the best in all of us, and the worst. Between crowded shopping, endless cooking, and hosting a variety of visiting relatives, many a normally rational person has been driven to desperation—sometimes even murder.

I'd been to the mall--something I don't relish in the best of times--and the holiday crowds, traffic, and surly temperament of my fellow shoppers had served to put me in a less than charitable mood. Rusty, our red-brown Lab greeted me at home with his usual I-love-you-no-matter-what exuberance. By the time I'd dropped my shopping bags on the sofa, shed my winter coat, and received a few doggy kisses from him, my attitude had begun to ease.

"Hey, you're home," Drake said, emerging from the kitchen. He carried the portable phone and extended it to me now. "Want to say hello to Mom?"

My mother-in-law and I haven't exactly established a rapport just yet. In the fourteen months I've been married to Drake I've met her only once, on a quick trip through Flagstaff, when we flew our helicopter there, on our way to a charter job at the Grand Canyon. During that visit, and a few other phone calls, she and I had probably not exchanged more than two hours worth of chit-chat. To be fair, the conversations had all been pleasant, with the only hint of coolness coming when she discovered that I hadn't taken the Langston name when I married her son. Drake was holding the phone out to me.

"Catherine! How are you?"

"Hi, Charlie—I'm doing just great. I'm so excited about the visit." She got high marks for her bubbly voice and general enthusiasm for life.

"Visit?" Somewhere in there I must have missed something.

"Oh, Drake didn't tell you yet? Well, we've decided that I'll come out there and spend Christmas week with you guys."

We have, huh. I glanced over at Drake but he'd gotten very busy scratching Rusty's ears.

"I can't wait," Catherine continued. "He tells me how

special New Mexico Christmases are, and I'm just dying to get in on some of the traditions."

I took a deep breath. "Well, we can't wait either," I said. "What day will you arrive?"

"The twentieth—that's the Friday before Christmas Day. I can stay a week. And Drake said I should bring Kinsey. Charlie, are you sure that's okay with you?"

Catherine's three year old blond cocker spaniel, named for her favorite mystery character, had been absolutely adorable when we'd visited their home. I felt sure she would be as well behaved when traveling and would get along with Rusty.

"Sure, she won't be any problem." I looked toward Drake again, but he'd disappeared into the kitchen. Catherine ended the phone call with love to all and I hung up, ready to track my husband.

"Your mother said thanks for the invitation," I told him when I found him at the kitchen sink, peeling potatoes for dinner.

He turned around sheepishly. "I hope you don't mind," he said. "It kind of popped out. See, she originally called to invite us to her place for Christmas. And, well, you know how it is with the helicopter service. I could get a call anytime and I can't really afford to leave town. So, I suggested she think about coming here instead. Guess I thought she'd take a few days to think about it and I could check with you in the meantime."

"It's okay. I mean, a little warning would have been better, but I don't mind. It'll give me a chance to get to know her better."

He pulled me into a hug. "You're terrific," he mumbled into my ear, giving a little nibble.

I pulled back to arm's length, eyeing the project on the kitchen counter. "So, what are those potatoes going to turn into?"

"Homemade French fries, smothered with chile and cheese?"

"Umm . . . consider yourself forgiven for anything at all." Drake makes the best homemade French fries ever.

I turned back toward the living room. "I think I finished the last of the shopping. I'm going to put all this stuff in the guest room. That way I'll be forced to finish wrapping it before your mom gets here." I mentally ticked off other things on my to-do list as I carried my bags into the newly remodeled section of the house, hoping I could fit it all into the following week. The baking for the annual neighborhood cookie swap could wait, as would the final touches on the luminarias for the yard decorations.

We live in the old Albuquerque Country Club neighborhood, and a big tradition in the city is that our neighborhood is decorated to the max so everyone else in town can drive through and stare at us. My parents did it when I was a kid and apparently the tradition goes back at least a generation beyond theirs. My neighbor to the south, Elsa Higgins, is like a surrogate grandmother to me and she's decorated her yard annually for the fifty-some years she's lived in that house. The tour thing has grown over the years. It used to be that folks just climbed into their cars and drove around. Now there are city bus tours, sold out weeks in advance, and the police place barricades so the tour can only follow certain streets—ours being one of them.

"Hon? Telephone." Drake handed the portable over to me. I hadn't even heard it ring. He shrugged to indicate that he didn't know who it was.

"Hello, Charlie, this is Judy. Judy Garfield. Next door."

Our newest neighbors, a couple of mild-mannered Midwesterners, had moved into the house north of ours two months earlier. The adjustment from life in one of the better suburbs of Chicago to the Southwest was coming as a bit of a culture shock to them.

"I just heard about the decoration requirements," she said. "I don't know what some of this stuff is."

It's probably only in the Southwest that a brown paper lunch sack, some sand, and a votive candle can be considered beautiful, but that's how we do it. I explained to her that they could either make their own or buy them ready-made and delivered from the Boy Scouts or other groups that sell them.

"Well . . .." She hesitated. "Wilbur is really getting into the holidays this year, with everything being so different and all. Could you show us how to make them?"

I added one more thing to my to-do list. "Sure. I think Drake wants to make ours too. We can have a lesson on it in the next few days."

We hung up after setting a time to work on luminarias the next afternoon. I closed the door to the guest room, leaving the pile of shopping bags in the middle of the bed, out of sight.

I changed from the wool slacks and fluffy sweater I'd worn shopping into jeans and a sweatshirt before rejoining Drake in the kitchen.

Rusty was supervising the dinner preparations, making sure any tidbits that fell to the floor were swiftly dispatched.

"Boy, those fries smell good," I told my husband, wrapping my arms around his middle and resting my face against his back. "Are they almost ready?"

"Five more minutes. I poured you some wine." He indicated a glass standing on the counter.

I sat at the kitchen table and took a sip while he stirred the green chile sauce simmering in a pan on the burner. I watched him pull the basket of fries out of the deep fryer and prop them on the side to drain. He set two dinner plates on the counter and reached for a bag of grated cheddar. Rusty whimpered but I managed not to.

"Forgot to tell you—Elsa called while you were out shopping."

"Busy day with the telephone, huh?"

"Wish they were business calls instead," he said. He divided the fried potatoes between the two plates, then shook the shredded cheese over them. It began to melt instantly against their heat. He ladled a good-sized dose of green chile sauce over the top of the heap, making a small mountain in the middle of each plate. I pulled flatware and napkins from a drawer and met him back at the table.

"Wow, am I ever hungry," I told him. "Braving the mall during the Christmas season is tough work."

"Hey, the least I could do is have dinner ready." he said. Shopping is not Drake's strong suit.

"I should probably get a little something extra for your mom, now that she'll be here," I said.

"I hope that was all right, my asking her without checking first."

"Just don't ever do it again," I teased, poking at him with a cheese coated French fry. "As punishment, you have to help with everything that needs to be done before Christmas." I told him about Judy's call and the planned sacks-and-sand operation for the next day.

"I'll go get the supplies," he promised. "And some spare light bulbs. Everything looked okay when I checked the strings in the garage this afternoon but it never hurts to have extras."

We usually decorate the house and trees with red bulbs, offset by the soft golden glow of the luminarias lining the sidewalks. When fire claimed part of our home over a year ago, we lost our supply of light strings but were, fortunately, able to replace them at last year's post-holiday sales.

We finished swabbing the sauce off our plates and Drake put the dishes in the dishwasher while I returned Elsa's phone call.

"So, red or green?" she asked, after we'd checked on each other's state of health.

"Green, of course," I told her. Not being much of a cook, I have my old favorite green chile stew recipe I fall back on every year for the annual Red and Green Chile Cookoff. New Mexico's two flavors of chile lend themselves so well to the holiday season that the cookoff has become an annual fund raiser for charity. Between my regular work as a partner at RJP Investigations and my occasional hand in Drake's helicopter service, I have to confess that there isn't much time to give back to the community. The holidays are one time when I make a little extra effort.

"The Cookoff is just a week from today," Elsa reminded.

"I think I'll do my grocery shopping tomorrow. Need anything?"

I gave her a short list of ingredients for my stew. Now that it looked as if we'd spend the upcoming weekend decorating the yard, time was about to become crunched. I'd also promised Ron at least two full days at the office next week, the gifts would need to be wrapped, the tree set up in the house, and Catherine would get here the same day I had to be down at the Convention Center cooking chile stew all day.

I glanced up at the wall calendar and noticed that today was Friday, the thirteenth.

Chapter 2

The sky turned white Monday morning and tiny grains of snow fluttered onto my windshield as I drove to the office. Sally, our part-time receptionist, was already there. Her car sat in the parking area behind the gray and white Victorian that houses the private investigation agency I own with my brother, Ron.

"Hey there," Sally greeted as Rusty and I blew in through the back door. "Weather's kind of taken a turn, hasn't it?" Her normally ruddy cheeks were pinker than usual but her shaggy blond haircut didn't look any more ruffled than it usually does.

"Whew! I'm just glad it wasn't doing this yesterday. We hung a hundred and forty-three strings of lights all over the outside of our house. Covered the trees with them too. And Saturday—I can't even begin to guess how many paper bag tops I folded down. Drake's got them all over the floor of the garage so he can fill them with sand over the next few days."

"By next year he'll probably be more than willing to buy them ready-made," she said with a chuckle.

"Who knows? He's very much a do-it-yourself kind of guy. And he offered to help the new neighbors with theirs, too. I don't think any of them knew what they were getting into."

"Ron's upstairs. Left his car off for an oil change and he wants you to take him out at lunchtime to pick it up. Looks like the only case in the works right now is one of those spouse-spying things. Can you imagine? Wanting to track your spouse during the holidays so you can get divorce ammo on him?"

I raised one eyebrow. Things people do to each other never cease to amaze me.

"Probably her way of saying 'Happy New Year!'." Sally finished stirring creamer into her coffee and headed back to her desk at the front of the converted old house.

I found my favorite mug and poured the last of the coffee from the pot, switching it off as I added sugar. Rusty stared expectantly up at the countertop, waiting for me to get him a biscuit from the tin we keep there.

Upstairs, I peeked through Ron's doorway and gave a little wave when I noticed he was already on the phone. He swears ninety percent of an investigator's work is done on the telephone and I'm beginning to believe it. I rarely see him without it pasted to his ear. In my own office across the hall, a stack of new mail awaited, which I quickly sorted by categories: bills to pay, letters to write, and circular file.

I was intent on entering expenses into the computer when I became aware of Ron standing in my doorway.

"Ready?" he asked.

"For what?"

"Sally said you'd take me downtown to get my car from the lube place. Hello? Remember?"

"Jeez, is it noon already?" I glanced at my watch and saw that it was.

"Time flies when you're having fun?"

I growled.

Rusty opted to stay at the office with Sally, who was microwaving a cup of hot chocolate. Thirty minutes later, I returned with a bag from McDonald's and the dog was more than happy to turn his affection back toward me. I was still intent on my fries when Sally came through, announcing that she was done for the day and going home to relieve her husband, Ross, of babysitting duties. I spent a couple of hours sending dunning notices to delinquent accounts and answering miscellaneous correspondence.

When I arrived back home, Drake had made little progress on the luminarias. He was slipping his jacket on as I took mine off.

"Got a call for a charter photo job," he said, brushing my lips with a quick kiss. "Been on the phone with this guy half the afternoon, planning the logistics of the thing. Wants to catch the sunset on the Sandias. I told him the light was terrible today, with this gray sky, but he wants to give it a try. Guess I'll buzz him around the west side for an hour or so. If he doesn't get decent pictures, the forecast is better for tomorrow and we'll try it again."

"Flight time?"

"No more than an hour. I'll call as I'm taking off."

The FAA requires a commercial aircraft to file a flight plan or provide someone within the company to monitor each flight. In Drake's business, that was me. I gave him a quick kiss and watched him drive away.

A faint tapping at the back door drew my attention.

"Got your groceries," Elsa said, coming into the kitchen. "The pork tenderloin looked wonderful. It's gonna make yours the winning stew."

I smiled and thanked her. Bless her heart, she has a lot more faith in my cooking abilities than I do. I heated a kettle and made us each a cup of tea. Drake called to give his takeoff time, which I jotted down, then Elsa and I settled back with our tea and several cookbooks to choose our recipes for the neighborhood cookie swap.

"Well, I'm doing my spritz," Elsa said, before we'd delved very far into the books. "They go over pretty good every year, especially the ones I decorate with those little candies."

"They're fabulous," I agreed. "Nothing like a cookie with tons of butter in it to get my loyalty."

I flipped aimlessly through the cookbook. "You know, I think I'll make biscochitos this year. They're Christmasy, and not nearly as much work as some of the frosted, decorated, fancy things other people bring."

"Oh, yes," she agreed enthusiastically, "those are wonderful. Do them."

I'd already filled her in on all the projects I had to accomplish within the week, and the fact that my mother-in-law would be here, now only three days away. We finished our tea and Elsa headed back to her house through the break in the hedge that's been there since I was a little girl. I used to duck out the kitchen door and try to get through the hedge before Mother could catch me and make me come back. Then I'd sit in Elsa's kitchen and be fed cookies and milk. When my parents died in a plane crash, Elsa Higgins took me into her home and kept me out of trouble until I could move back into the family home and be on my own. Anyone who'll take in a teenager for a couple of years should probably have "Saint" stenciled above her doorway.

I flipped aimlessly through the cookbooks for a few more minutes but didn't change my mind about my choice. Drake phoned to say he'd landed and I noticed that the gray day was dying, becoming a gray twilight.

The next two days flew by, filled with gift wrapping, freshening the guest room, and setting up the tree in the living room. By Friday morning, I'd made about all the preparations I could for a mother-in-law visit. I gathered my ingredients for green chile stew and headed downtown to the Convention Center and the cookoff. The plan was that Catherine would arrive about mid-afternoon and Drake would bring her downtown to sample the results.

I was well into dipping out my four hundredth ladle of stew into someone's Styrofoam bowl when I glanced up to see my husband grinning at me. Next to him, Catherine stood regal as ever, her sleek page perfect and her makeup freshly retouched. I pictured how I must look--wilted hair, sweaty upper lip, and tomato stains on my white apron. Makeup isn't something I do much with anyway—a touch of lipstick and maybe mascara on a good day—so I knew that department was lacking.

Catherine waited until my customers walked away, then she came over to gather me into a hug.

"Charlie, you look great!" she greeted.

My expression must have shown my skepticism.

"Well, okay, not the *best*, but really, dear, I'm so glad to see you."

I took the compliment as graciously as possible.

"Can we have a taste?" Drake said, eyeing the nearly-empty pot.

"Did you buy a ticket? Gotta have your official tasting bowl, you know."

He produced two of the generic Styrofoam bowls and I gave them each a dipper full. He rolled his eyes as he tasted; my green chile stew is his favorite dish.

"Charlie, this is wonderful," Catherine exclaimed. "Really, really good. I vote for it to be the winner."

I had to chuckle. "You haven't tried any of the others yet," I said.

"That's okay—I still vote for yours."

I smiled at her. "Doesn't look like there's going to be any left to take home. Otherwise, we could have it for dinner."

"Looks like we'll just have to go to Pedro's," Drake said, shrugging his shoulders. Like eating out at our favorite little spot was a big sacrifice.

I glanced at my watch. "Cookoff's over in another fifteen minutes," I told them. "If you want to check out the other booths before everything's gone, go ahead."

"I think I'll save space for Pedro's," Drake said. "Need help carrying anything out to the car?"

I gathered most of the utensils and ingredients I hadn't used and let him carry them away. Catherine wandered down the long row of booths while I finished wiping up a few stray spills. The crowd had thinned considerably.

"Looks like they raised quite a lot for the homeless," Catherine said, coming back.

"Good. I'm glad it helped. This event has become quite a tradition. Gets bigger every year."

Drake came back and carried the remaining gear outside and I folded my apron. Fifteen minutes later we were parking both vehicles in front of Pedro's tiny establishment near Old Town. The little parking lot only contained three other vehicles, making it nearly full.

Inside, three of the six tables were occupied, one by Mannie, a grizzled old man who eats chile hotter than most people can stand. He raised his gray-speckled chin in greeting as we took our usual table in the corner.

Concha, Pedro's other half, was in the process of setting heaping plates of tacos on one table. "Margaritas?" she asked as we passed.

"Three," Drake said.

Pedro stood behind the bar, whirring the cool green drinks in his blender. Concha wiped her hands on her apron and picked up the glasses. Balancing a small cocktail tray, she threaded her way toward our table. Drake introduced his mother and the Spanish woman gave Catherine a warm smile.

"I thought you were getting a waitress," I asked her as she set my drink down.

She made a sound that came out like "Pah!" and pulled out her order pad. "Kids. Can't get any of them to do any work. Easier to do it myself."

I noticed that Pedro had headed back to the kitchen while she wrote down our order. Easy enough, since Drake and I usually have the same thing—chicken enchiladas with sour cream. Green. Catherine followed suit.

"I'd forgotten how you get a choice of red or green chile here in New Mexico," Catherine said after Concha had left. "Most places any more make up these weird concoctions called sauce, and you really don't know what kind of chile is in it."

I could tell I was going to get along just fine with her.

Chapter 3

Sunday morning dawned clear and cold. Frost was thick on the grass and trees, but the hoped-for snowfall from a few days ago seemed to have vanished. Albuquerque rarely gets snow for Christmas—only an inch or two when we do--and it was looking like this year would be no exception.

"Is there more cinnamon, Charlie?" Catherine was helping me bake the biscochitos and we were running out of the cinnamon-sugar coating we'd mixed up earlier.

"Check that upper cabinet," I told her. "I'm pretty sure we're not out."

So far the co-baking project was going along fine. We had two good-sized batches of the traditional Mexican cookies almost done. Catherine and I worked well together in the kitchen, with Rusty and Kinsey supervising as only dogs can. The big red Lab and the little cocker both sat with ears perked and deep brown eyes staring winsomely at our every move.

The cookie swap is our neighborhood's way of getting together socially for an afternoon and for everyone to take home a variety of holiday cookies without having to bake for days on end. Later this afternoon we'd all meet at the Country Club and have a couple of glasses of sinfully rich eggnog and indulge in far too many calories. I couldn't wait.

Drake eased into the kitchen and slipped one star-shaped cookie from the cooling rack.

"Uh-uh," I scolded. "You're supposed to come to the party to get some."

"That doesn't make any sense," he complained. "You're going to bring home a box full anyway. Why can't I just have some now?"

I shot him a look.

"Besides, I probably won't be able to go. That photographer who got lousy gray pictures the other day wants to try again this afternoon now that the sky's cleared. Looks like I may have to be out with him most of the afternoon." He tried his best to look underfed, so I gave him another cookie and was rewarded with his gorgeous smile and a kiss.

"By the way," he said, "did you notice some guy cruising

the street in a dark blue car awhile ago? Thought he might
be casing the place, so I took down his license number." He
reached into his pocket and pulled out a scrap of paper.

The phone rang, interrupting.

"Charlie? It's Judy. Judy Garfield. Next door."

I wondered if she'd continue to identify herself so
completely every single time she called. I stuck Drake's note to
the refrigerator with a daisy-shaped magnet.

"The cookie swap this afternoon? Is it okay to bring a
guest?" Judy asked.

"Sure. Catherine's coming with me. Drake may not be able
to make it."

I could hear her taking a deep breath on the other end.
"Well, Wilbur's mother dropped in, and we'd like to bring her if
that's all right."

"Really? You hadn't said anything about having company
for the holidays. That's nice she could make it." I brushed sugar
off my hands. "I'm sure it's no problem to bring her along.
We'll see you there—about four?"

"See you then." Her voice sounded tight, like she was
talking with her teeth clenched.

* * *

The Country Club's dining room was dressed in all its holiday finery when we arrived. Twin spruce trees at each end of the room were laden with bows, pinecones, and bunches of sugared fruit. Red and gold satin ribbons draped the cookie tables, set up along three walls. Already, platters of cookies filled two of the long tables, beckoning with their loads of butter and sugar. I set my plates down and turned to see who was already here.

Elsa stood across the room, a dainty basket hanging from her arm, her puff of white hair freshly styled. She seemed intent on a plate of some kind of cookie with bright red maraschino cherries in the centers.

"Let's go say hello," I invited Catherine.

"Oh, that's your neighbor, isn't it? The one who's also your grandmother."

"Almost—that's right."

Elsa remembered Catherine immediately. "And where's that husband of yours?" she asked me.

"Got a flight and couldn't make it. He'll consume his share of the cookies later, I'm sure."

A commotion at the entry grabbed our attention.

"Oh! I'm so sorry," a woman was saying. Her voice came through the room clearly, as though amplified. "Judy, here let me get that."

I looked beyond her to see Judy Garfield, looking mortified, standing just inside the vestibule.

"Judy! Did you hear me? I said I'll take that for you."

Unfortunately, everyone in the room heard her and all eyes were watching the little scene play out. Judy and Wilbur each carried a heavy-looking platter covered with plastic wrap and the woman was attempting to take a plate in each hand, something that clearly was not a good idea. Wilbur said something quietly into her ear and she finally settled for carrying only one of the platters.

She tottered into the dining room on red four-inch heels. The shoes were complimented by a strapless red satin dress, formfitted to the waist then blossoming out in a tulip shaped skirt. Her short-short black hair was pulled back on the right side and held in place by a monster of a red poinsettia. The whole effect was a bit much for a neighborhood gathering at four o'clock on a Sunday afternoon.

I was beginning to figure out why Judy's voice had sounded so tense this morning.

Wilbur placed a guiding hand on his mother's elbow and ushered her toward the tables at the far right wall. Judy followed meekly, looking as if she wished the floor would swallow her up. As Wilbur and the red woman set their platters down, all eyes stayed on that end of the room and conversation had not quite picked up again.

"Well," said Elsa. "That's certainly interesting."

Catherine and I both chuckled at her estimation of the situation.

I caught Judy's eye and gave a little wave. She smiled and practically trotted across the room toward us. She wore a gray pleated skirt and gray and pink sweater. Her straight brown hair was pulled back with a pink headband.

"Your mother-in-law?" I asked hesitantly, nodding toward the other end of the room.

"Oh yes." Her eyelids dropped for a moment, as if she had a headache.

"She's certainly colorful," Elsa offered.

"Oh yes," Judy said again. "That she is."

Wilbur had spotted us and was steering his mother in our direction. His scalp blushed extra pink through his thinning, sandy hair. As they approached, I noticed that the woman was really rather petite, no more than five-two, even in the high heels. Her hair was deep black and her brows were penned in to be the same color. Lipstick the same shade as the satin dress served to highlight the fact that there were deep creases beside her mouth, and the crow's feet at her eyes were the kind caused by heavy smoking.

Wilbur spoke up. "This is my mother, Paula Candelaria."

"Charlie! I'm just so *glad* to meet you," she squawked as he introduced me. "Judy's told me so much *about* you. A private *eye*—that must be so *exciting!*"

Her voice came out at least a dozen decibels louder than anyone else's. Heads turned again.

"Well," I murmured, purposely bringing my own voice lower, "I'm not really a private investigator. Just a partner in the firm."

"But you solve *mur*ders and *every*thing," she went on, not taking my hint to lower her voice.

I shrugged, scrambling vainly for another subject. "That

eggnog sure looks good," I suggested.

Paula's head whipped toward the end of the long table. "Oh, my, yes. That does look good. I sure hope they made it strong enough."

She began a sprint toward the opposite end of the room and stumbled in her spiky heels. Mr. Delacourte, a Methodist minister who lived two streets over from us, reached out instinctively to catch her elbow. She turned and placed both hands against his chest.

"Why *thank* you, kind sir. You saved me from embarrassing myself."

Mrs. Delacourte turned three shades whiter and I could swear I heard her sharp intake of breath.

Mr. Delacourte removed Paula's hands from his lapels and mumbled some kind of gracious reply.

Paula turned with a swish of her red tulip skirt and headed again for the punchbowl. I caught myself holding my breath as I watched her maneuver the ladle shakily toward her cup.

Beside me, Judy took a deep breath and squeezed her eyes shut. Wilbur headed to the end of the cookie table, where gold boxes with tissue linings waited for residents to fill with their choices of goodies to take home. Conversation in the room began to return to normal and Elsa had resumed her browsing.

"I'm so sorry," Judy murmured. "I had no idea she'd make such a scene. I suspect she got into Wilbur's special cognac before we left the house."

"Hey, it's not your fault," I assured her. "Is she going to be staying through Christmas?" I tried to make the question sound polite.

"Ugh, yes. I hope I make it."

"Judy, I don't want to sound rude, but is she always like this?"

Her eyes rolled. "Her behavior is very off-and-on. It's just that it's been 'off' much more frequently since she left husband number five a few months ago. I just had this feeling, this dreadful feeling, that she'd show up and want to spend the holidays with us.

"See, she latches onto Wilbur in every crisis. In our twelve years of marriage, she's been through two husbands and I can't even guess how many boyfriends. It'd be sad if I could watch it from a distance, but every time she lands on our doorstep I just grit my teeth."

"You're right—it is sad," I sympathized.

"And now, with the baby, I just don't want her around. Can you imagine how you'd feel if she were your grandmother?"

"A baby? Judy, you didn't tell me!"

She blushed. "Well, we've wanted this for so long and had a couple of miscarriages. I hadn't planned to make it public until I get a little farther along."

"It's okay, I won't tell anyone—except Drake. Would that be okay?" I reached for a cut-out Santa on a platter near me. "Does Paula know?"

"No! Sorry. I really don't want her to find out yet. I just hope Wilbur can keep it quiet awhile longer."

A crash and the tinkle of breaking glass grabbed our attention. Paula stood at the punchbowl, ladle in hand.

"Hey! Watch it, lady." The abrasive male voice came from Chuck Ciacarelli, one of the richest men in town with a reputation for being nasty tempered. We called him Chuckie Cheese behind his back.

Paula was staring at the floor with a puzzled expression. Two women nearby knelt to pick up broken glass, while another reached for a handful of napkins.

"Careful, you're bleeding," the napkin woman said.

"Oh, my gosh," I said to Judy, "it looks like Paula's cut her hand."

"At this rate we'll be lucky if she doesn't kill herself," Wilbur said, handing Judy his partially-filled cookie box and heading toward his mother.

"Or lucky if she does," muttered Judy.

Chapter 4

I gazed out at the early morning, trying to determine whether it was cloudy or merely too early for the sky to show any color yet. Christmas Eve. It was going to be a busy day and I really wanted nothing more than to snuggle in with Drake and wake up three days later to find the holiday hoopla all behind me.

We'd spent all day Monday setting the luminarias along the sidewalks and driveways. Paula had been much subdued after her antics at the cookie swap Sunday afternoon. Drake and I pitched in and set Elsa's sacks out for her and then helped Judy and Wilbur do the last of theirs. A plan had evolved that the three households would get together for dinner tonight, then we'd go out and look at the lights.

One downside of living in the most popular section of town for Christmas light displays is that the police barricade our streets off and the traffic is so solidly packed that there's no hope of getting out of our own driveway anytime after late afternoon. We've learned over the years to settle in and plan on Christmas Eve at home. I decided to make another batch of my green chile stew, since Drake had hardly gotten a taste of the last one. It could easily feed the whole group. Elsa would contribute cornbread and Judy planned to bring a salad. Paula said something about making eggnog, but Judy quietly nixed that. Paula without alcohol would definitely be easier to handle.

I nestled into Drake's shoulder for a few more minutes but finally decided I was too wide-awake to actually get any more rest. I kissed his bare chest and rolled off the bed. Ten minutes later, quick-showered, dressed, and with a hasty swipe of the hairbrush, I padded to the kitchen in my socks. Rusty trotted along and Kinsey, hearing him in the hallway, nosed the guestroom door open and followed us.

I let the two dogs out into the back yard while I started coffee. By the time it finished trickling into the carafe, Catherine had emerged from her room, hair freshly brushed, wearing a cozy burgundy velour robe. We good-morninged each other while I pulled two mugs from the cupboard.

"I hope I don't live to regret my offer to Paula," she said, taking her mug and adding a slight drizzle of cream.

Catherine, with the patience of a saint, had offered to take Paula shopping for a few last-minute things. They planned to leave shortly after breakfast this morning and come back mid-afternoon.

"I'll watch Kinsey while I make the stew," I offered. "Or maybe it's the other way around."

"I think you've got that right. Once she smells something cooking, she'll be right in your face."

"It's okay. I'm used to it. She's such a little sweetheart. Easy to have around." I opened the kitchen door and the dogs raced in. They both headed for the food dishes I'd set out.

Catherine and I toasted a couple of English muffins and finished our coffee.

"Guess I better get dressed. The sooner we hit the stores, the sooner we'll get back," she said.

Drake shuffled into the kitchen wearing pajama bottoms I'd never seen before and his favorite old robe. Catherine gave her son a quick kiss and headed toward her room. I gave him a much longer kiss and settled him at the table with a mug of coffee.

"Woo-hoo! Anybody home?" Paula poked her head into the kitchen.

I shot Drake a look. He shrugged and held up the newspaper he'd carried in. *Yeah*, I tried to convey, *you forgot to relock the door.*

"Coffee! I smell coffee," chirped Paula. "Do you mind?" She'd already begun opening cabinet doors, looking for the cups.

I handed her a clean one.

"Judy and Wilbur don't drink coffee," she said. "Can you believe it? God, I can't believe there's a household in America where they don't make coffee in the morning."

She took a long sip and let out a satisfied sigh. "Man, I needed that." She settled into the chair across from Drake and reached for his newspaper. My husband is too well-mannered to actually swat her hand, but I could tell the temptation was there.

Paula wore a skin-tight pair of black jeans, high heeled boots, and a fluffy sweater in a bright shade of magenta. Her short black hair was slicked back from her forehead with some kind of gel and would have looked model-like except for the patch in back that still had a little sleep tangle in it.

"Catherine's getting ready now," I told Paula. "She mentioned that you were going shopping this morning."

"Yeah, silly me." She did a little forehead knock with the heel of her hand. "Here I show up at Christmas without any gifts. When I saw all the stuff Wilbur and Judy have under their tree, well, duh, figured I better get with the program."

"I'm sure they weren't really expecting much," I offered gently. *Least of all were they expecting you to show up unannounced.*

"Guess I've just had a few other things on my mind. This hasn't been an easy year, I'll tell you. Divorce. That's really hit me hard." Her voice had turned from perky to teary in an instant. "And my job—huh, that's a joke. *Downsized*, they're calling it. Truth is, they're cutting out everybody who might be getting close to collecting any of their precious retirement fund."

She took another deep sip of her coffee.

"Hah! Guess that'll teach me to trust those corporate types." A cackle started down in her throat and turned nearly hysterical on its way to her lips. "Lucky I had kids to come home to."

I glanced at Drake. He was intently studying the stock market pages.

"Um, maybe I should let Catherine know you're here." I refilled her mug and dashed toward the bedrooms.

"Gosh, are the stores even open yet?" Catherine asked after I tapped on her door.

"Take your time," I said. "I can always send her back to Judy's for awhile."

When I got back into the kitchen, Paula was rummaging through my refrigerator. "Got any jam?"

I pointed to the jars sitting in the racks on the door. I noticed that she'd helped herself to a couple of slices of bread, which were browning in the toaster oven. Drake had abandoned his newspaper, probably deciding to get dressed and find something to do outside. The dogs were sitting in front of the toaster, their bright-eyed gazes traveling between the food and Paula. She didn't appear to notice them.

I busied myself rinsing Drake's mug and putting a few things into the dishwasher. Paula made herself comfortable at the table with her toast and our newspaper.

"Are you thinking about staying here in Albuquerque?"

I asked. A quick image flashed through my mind of Paula coming over early every morning, helping herself to my coffee, some breakfast, and our newspaper. I dropped a knife into the sink with a clatter.

"Hmm? Oh, I don't know yet," she answered. "Maybe sometime after New Year's I'll start checking out the want ads."

Poor Judy.

Catherine came in, dressed in a pair of tailored gray wool slacks and a deep blue sweater that gave a rich tone to her sleek, dark hair. She took in the scene and raised an eyebrow toward me. Paula mumbled a "good morning" through a mouthful of toast and turned back to the horoscope section of the paper.

"Well," said Catherine, trying to work some cheerfulness into her voice. "I guess we could get going anytime."

Paula brushed crumbs off her hands onto her jeans and stood, leaving her plate and mug beside the rumpled newspaper.

"Don't worry about those dishes, Paula. I'll get them." Like she'd planned on cleaning them up. As they left, I glanced up at the clock. She'd been here a whole twenty minutes. It was going to be a long week.

Chapter 5

Drake was busily checking the outdoor lights once more when I opened the front door to look for him. The sky had turned white again, an ominous indicator that there might be snow later in the day.

"Hon, I think those bulbs haven't had time to burn out yet," I teased.

"It wasn't the bulbs I was saving," he said, peeking around the huge blue spruce by the dining room window.

"Your mother is really a doll. Anyone who would voluntarily spend a day shopping with Paula . . ."

He walked toward the front porch and put his arms around my waist. His face was red and chilly. "Hey, do you realize we're alone? For probably the only time this week."

"Uh, not exactly." I spotted Judy Garfield walking across the lawn toward us, bundled up in wool slacks and a puffy car coat.

He groaned, dropped one arm, and turned to face her.

"Oh, Charlie, I'm sorry Paula came over so early this morning," she began. "I thought she was still in her room—it takes her forever to get dressed and made up in the mornings."

"It's okay. Catherine was almost ready." I glanced up at Drake, who was eyeing the neatly placed luminarias along the sidewalk.

A dark blue car cruised by, the driver looking at addresses. I got an impression of a male with longish dark hair and wraparound sunglasses. When he realized the three of us were staring at him, he sped up and took a left at the intersection. I glanced toward Drake, but he was still staring after the car.

Without a jacket, I was feeling the chill in the air. I'd ask him about it later. I turned to Judy. "Want some coffee—or how about a cup of tea?"

"Tea would be great," she said, pushing a wisp of mousy hair behind her ear.

In the kitchen, I set a kettle on the burner and found two muffins left from earlier in the week. I gathered the scattered newspapers into a relatively neat pile and set mugs and tea bags out. Judy slumped into one of the chairs.

"I tell you, Charlie, I'm whipped," she sighed. "Having Paula around is like inviting a tornado into your home. She's a bundle of constant energy, the kind that needs to be the center of attention. And the phone rings constantly for her. What did she do—tell everyone she knows that she's visiting us?"

I didn't mention Paula's comment about possibly making it more than a visit.

"Course, I guess that also describes what having a child must be like," she laughed. "Maybe this is good practice for me."

"Well, at least a baby starts out small and unable to get into everything," I offered. "You have a little time to get used to it."

She dunked her teabag four times and wrung it out by twisting the string around a spoon. Laying the wet bag on a saucer, she began to peel the paper off a muffin.

"I'll tell you, though," she said, her eyes narrowing to slits. "I won't *ever* get used to having Paula around. Wilbur won't do anything about her. He's . . . well, she's ingrained a lot of intimidation into him. But I will. And pretty soon."

I sipped my tea and watched her rip the muffin paper into tiny shreds.

* * *

By four o'clock that afternoon I'd stuffed the last of the packages under the tree, helped Drake straighten the luminaria sacks, and had the pot of green chile stew simmering on the stove. Catherine had come home around three, looking somewhat frazzled. She'd opted for a nap before the evening festivities and, thinking that sounded like a pretty good idea, I crawled onto our bed and pulled a quilt over myself.

Drake's gentle hand on my shoulder woke me. "Hey, you gonna sleep all night?" he teased.

I mumbled something incoherent.

"Elsa just showed up at the back door with corn bread, and I have a feeling the others might arrive any time."

"Oh, my god, what time is it anyway?"

"Almost six."

I realized the windows were dark and couldn't believe I'd slept nearly two hours. I whipped the quilt aside and stood up too fast.

"Take it easy," he said. "I turned on the outdoor lights. Cars are already coming up the street. The stew is doing fine, and Mom and I set the table in the dining room. I think everything's under control."

The doorbell rang. "Uh-oh, get that, okay? I'll brush my teeth real quick and get the tangles out of my hair."

He blew me a kiss from the doorway. "No rush."

I emerged five minutes later to a houseful of people. Catherine was setting food on the table and Drake had managed to satisfy everyone's needs drink-wise. I slipped past Judy (looking a little tense around the mouth) and Paula (dressed in green leather pants, a tight red sweater, and red flats) and made my way to the kitchen. Tasted the stew, just to be sure it had turned out all right, before we began ladling it into bowls.

"How did the shopping trip go today?" I asked Catherine, keeping my voice low.

"Interesting."

"Just—interesting?"

"Well, I'll tell you, I learned more about Paula that I ever wanted to know. She gave me the whole lowdown on what was wrong with each of the five ex-husbands, and a few juicy tidbits about some new young hunk she's seeing."

"Oh boy, I'll bet that was fun."

She rolled her eyes and began carrying the bowls of hot stew into the dining room. I followed with another batch and called everyone to the table. I noticed that Catherine chose to sit by Drake's side at one end, staying as far from Paula's chair as possible. Wilbur sat near Paula, probably at Judy's insistence, although from what she'd told me, if Paula got out of hand Wilbur would be the last person to do anything about it. Judy seated herself on the other side of her husband, undoubtedly for the close proximity to his shins.

Actually, dinner went quite well, with Elsa entertaining us with stories of Christmases in the '50s. When she got to the point where she was about to reveal some of my crazier antics as a kid, it looked like a good time to start our tour of the neighborhood lights.

While I have to admit that having the neighborhood barricaded and watching bumper-to-bumper traffic snake its way down our street until the wee hours of the morning doesn't sound like an appealing way to spend Christmas Eve, we local residents have discovered a nice side benefit. We get to slip behind the barricades and walk the closed-off streets, enjoying a private show of our own.

"Looks like it could snow a bit," Drake said, peering out between the bedroom drapes as I slipped on heavy socks and walking boots. "That sky's awfully white."

"Better caution everyone to bundle up," I said, remembering Paula's attire.

Out in the living room, everyone had put on heavy coats, gloves and caps. Rusty and Kinsey were waiting by the door expectantly.

I eyed Paula's leather slacks and thin leather flats without socks. "Paula, I'd be happy to loan you some sweats and some socks," I offered.

"Oh, thanks, Charlie, but that's okay. I'll be fine in these." Her chic winter jacket of red faux fur just wouldn't have been the thing with sweats, I guess.

I clipped a leash on Rusty's collar, and Catherine did the same with Kinsey. By default, because we were being dragged ahead by the dogs, she and I ended up leading the little procession. I glanced back to see Drake lock the front door behind him, then offer Elsa an assisting hand on her elbow.

We walked past Elsa's house and the next one, holding our

breath against the exhaust of the tour buses. At the corner, we turned left, slipping past a barricade that kept traffic off the side street as well as two other blocks behind ours. By the time we were one street over from our own, the difference was incredible. The traffic noises and smells faded away and we strolled leisurely down the middle of the streets enjoying our own private show of all the homes not on the regular tour.

Catherine exclaimed over the number of luminarias lining the sidewalks and driveways. "I can't imagine how much work went into all this," she said. "And the lights, look how beautiful they are!"

"Oops!" cried Paula. "I sure didn't see that crack in the street."

Wilbur reached out and grasped his mother's arm, steadying her. I wondered how many martinis she'd made for herself after the one Drake had given her. I reined Rusty in and held him back until Drake caught up with us. He slipped his arm around my shoulders.

"Merry Christmas, sweetheart," I whispered to him. No matter how crazy the rest of the holiday got, I was glad we had each other.

"Hey, look," he said. "Told you it looked like snow."

A big, fat white flake drifted in front of me and landed on Rusty's back. Soon, there were thousands of them and the street had a thin white cover. I smiled, remembering Drake's and my first Christmas together last year at the Taos Ski Valley. There'd certainly been no shortage of snow there. I tilted my face up to the sky and let the flakes land on my eyelids. I would ignore Paula and do my best not to get involved with my neighbors' problems.

Well it was a good intention, anyway.

Chapter 6

I awoke to gray light filtering around the edges of the drapes and utter silence outside. My first thought was: the buses have gone away. I rolled toward Drake and he pulled me into his arms. The next thing I knew he was planting little nibbles along my neck and shoulder and the rest became a pleasant blur of sensation as we pulled the covers over ourselves and enjoyed each other.

I awoke for the second time to a brighter gray light. I reached for Drake again, but he wasn't there.

"Snowed about three inches," he whispered, emerging from the bathroom.

"Really?" I was instantly awake and wanting to go out and play in it. He pulled me back into his arms and wrapped the comforter around both of us.

Rusty sat by the edge of the bed, signaling that he'd soon require attention. We ignored him.

"I'll make breakfast if you want to go out there and build a snowman or something," Drake said. "I can tell you're itching to get up."

"Well . . . if you're sure." I was up and rummaging in the closet for my ski pants almost before he'd finished the offer.

He laughed out loud and tossed a pillow at me. I dashed into the bathroom and brushed my teeth in record time, then slipped into ski pants and boots.

"C'mon, Rust, we're gonna have some fun."

I heard water running in the guest bath, so I opened Catherine's bedroom door and let Kinsey dash out. "You too," I told her. "We're gonna play!"

The two dogs beat me to the back door by a longshot and bounded ahead of me. Kinsey leaped through the fresh powder, her stubby little tail pointing straight up. Rusty made his usual rounds of all the trees and sniffed to make sure intruder dogs hadn't used them during the night. I packed a bit of the powder and tried for a snowball, but it was pretty hopeless. The stuff was dry as shredded cotton. I had to be happy with running around the yard, tossing handfuls of white powder at the two dogs and watching them try to bite at it as it hit their heads.

"Breakfast!" Drake called from the doorway. He batted at the dogs' fur with an old towel, knocking the powdery white off them. Kinsey had loads of it imbedded in the long blond hair around her legs and belly and in her long, curly ears.

"Your cheeks are red," he said to me.

"Umm, feels good. Don't worry about the dogs—they can't hurt the kitchen tile too badly."

An hour later, we'd finished a fabulous breakfast of eggs Benedict and fresh fruit and were well into the loot under the tree in the living room. Catherine had given us matching robes and Drake gave me a heart-shaped diamond pendant and my very own .380 automatic. He'd been teaching me to shoot at our local range where I usually used his 9 mm Beretta. This would be lighter to handle and small enough I could carry it in my purse. My gift to him was a set of aviation references— lacking the romantic element, but something he'd been wanting for a long time. Together, our gift to Catherine was a vacation trip she'd been wanting to take to visit her elderly aunt in Vermont. Drake had told me that Aunt Ruthie was a real pistol at eight-nine years old, but just couldn't quite manage a two-thousand-mile-long journey.

"This is the best," Drake sighed, plopping himself on the couch, gazing fondly at his mother and then at me, while stroking one of the reference books in his lap. I wasn't sure which of the above made him the happiest, but it didn't really matter. I stretched out in one recliner and Catherine took the other. I had an instant's déjà vu as I remembered holidays in this same room when I was a kid.

"Well, if we're going to have turkey tonight, I think I better put it in the oven," I finally said, pulling myself out of my little haven.

The phone rang just as I walked into the kitchen.

"Merry Christmas, Charlie." It was Judy. "If you're not terribly busy right now, could I come over for a minute?"

"Sure. We're pretty much just laying around, fat and happy," I told her. With eggs Benedict for breakfast and a full turkey dinner coming up—fat and happy was a pretty good description.

A couple of minutes later, I heard Drake open the front door then Judy came into the kitchen.

"Thanks so much," she breathed, sinking into one of the

kitchen chairs. "I just had to get out for a little while."

"Coffee?" I offered, belatedly remembering that she didn't drink it.

"Please. Strong."

I raised an eyebrow. "I could make you some tea, if you'd rather."

She waved her hand back and forth. "No, it's okay, really."

She accepted the mug I handed over and doused it liberally with sugar and cream while I put the turkey into the roasting pan and set it in the oven.

"You don't look like you're having such a great day," I offered tentatively.

She made a low growling sound. "Oh, it started off all right. Paula was so hung over from last night—apparently she'd restocked her hidden supply and managed to duck into her room several times throughout the evening. Anyway, she slept til nearly eleven this morning and Wilbur and I finally had some time to ourselves."

She sipped at the coffee and grimaced. "The fun started after that. She came dragging into the kitchen and informed us that she plans to stay in Albuquerque and that she'll be living with us until she gets a job and a place of her own. Not more than a couple of months—" Her voice cracked and she put her forehead on the table. A sound came out that sounded like "no, no, no."

"Staying?" I'm afraid my own voice sounded frightened.

Judy raised her head. Her eyes were red rimmed, her face blotchy. "I can't handle it, Charlie, I really can't." She raised the coffee mug and put it back down. "And the worst part is that Wilbur won't say anything. He doesn't want her here either. We've talked about this when we're alone. But he just can't stand up to her."

I microwaved a new mug of water and got out a tea bag.

"Here. I don't think that coffee's doing you much good."

She did the dunking and squeezing ritual and took a sip before she spoke again. "What am I going to do?"

"Change the locks? Move to Zimbabwe?" I offered helpfully.

"Have plastic surgery so she won't recognize me?"

"Go into the Witness Protection Program?"

"Bump her off?"

"But only in the most painful way possible."

"Oh yes, only that would do." She giggled and took a good pull on her tea. "I better get going. I've got a few things to do around the house and I'd love a nap. Wilbur and I are invited to a dinner party tonight. And Paula's *not* going."

"Hey, at least we put a smile back on your face," I said. I walked her to the front door and watched her move lightly down the steps. The sun had come out early and melted the snow from walkways and street, leaving only the lawns and shrubs in frosty white.

A nap sounded pretty good to me too, but I first called each of my brothers to wish them Merry Christmas. Paul's household in Mesa, Arizona, was raucous with the shrieks of his two kids and a series of electronic blips in the background. Distracted by all of it, Paul was clearly not with me, so I ended the call after just the basics. Ron answered his phone with a note of hope in his voice.

"Oh, I thought it might be the boys," he said when he heard my voice.

"They'll call," I assured him. My heart goes out to my elder brother every other year when he faces this separation from his kids. Part of the price one pays for selecting the wrong spouse, then producing three munchkins before figuring out what kind of person she really is. Ron's divorce hit him hard and Bernadette did nothing to make it easier, either for him or for the kids.

"Dinner's at five," I told him, repeating the invitation extended a few days earlier. "But come any time. You and Drake can play with your new Christmas toys." I didn't mention my new gun. Knowing my brother, he'd convince Drake to head out to the range immediately, and I wanted to be the first to fire it. Sometime in the next few days we'd find the time.

I awoke to the weird sensation that something was way out of place. Before my eyes opened, the realization came that there were voices. I rolled over and moaned and squinted at the red numerals on my bedside clock. 12:37. No wonder—I was still into those first few really deep-sleep hours. After our early dinner, we'd sat around the table playing card games for several hours before calling it a night around eleven.

The voices rose and fell and seemed to be coming from outside.

"What's going on?" Drake said, his voice coming through clearly, like he'd been awake for awhile.

I turned toward him and realized that I was seeing faint images of red and blue lights swirling across the ceiling. I swung my legs over the edge of the bed and slipped on my new robe. Stepping to the window, I peeked into the back yard. Same eerie swirling lights, but no clue as to their source. I stepped into our bathroom, whose windows face the side yard and the Garfield's house. The strobes were clearly reflecting off the side of their home.

"Something's wrong next door," I told Drake. "Let me see."

I nearly tripped over Rusty as he jumped up and tried to race me to the hall. Drake was pulling on his robe as I made my way through the darkened house to the front door. I gripped Rusty's collar as I opened the front door and stepped out to the front porch.

Three police cars sat at the curb in front of the Garfield's house and ours. An ambulance was backed into Wilbur and Judy's driveway. It was the vehicle with the lights flashing. A small cluster of neighbors stood in front of the Johnson's, the house directly across from ours. Luminaria bags slumped in wilted mounds along their sidewalk.

"What's going on?" Drake said, joining me on our front porch.

"Can't tell. Something next door. Gotta get shoes," I gasped. My bare feet were nearly frozen to the cement.

I ran back inside and dropped my robe, pulling on jeans and a sweatshirt, socks and my walking boots. Drake was right behind me, grabbing clothes and boots, too. I instructed Rusty that he had to stay inside and I headed across the lawn toward the Garfield's front door.

"Hold it right there, ma'am," a sharp voice commanded. A rough hand gripped my shoulder and spun me around. "Charlie?"

"Kent? What's going on here?"

He dropped his hand but stood firmly blocking my way.

"This is a crime scene. Neighbors of yours, I gather?"

"Uh, yeah. I live right here," I said, indicating our house with a vague wave. "What kind of crime?" I knew it was a stupid question the minute it slipped out. Kent Taylor only worked one kind of case—homicide.

Chapter 7

W ho . . .?" My mind couldn't come up with anything more intelligent at the moment. I felt Drake walk up beside me and was aware that Taylor greeted him by name.

He consulted his notes. "A Paula Candelaria," he said. "Not a resident of the home, visiting her son and daughter-in-law."

"Right." Paula was dead? It took me a minute to process it. Then the floodgates opened and a thousand thoughts rushed through. *Couldn't happen to a nicer person. At least she can't move in and take over Judy's life now. What a pain she's been. What a pitiful person, so desperate for attention, her drinking out of control . . .* I found myself staring at the ground, waffling between feelings of relief that she was gone and horror that I would think that way.

"Do you . . .?"

I realized that Kent Taylor had said something to me and I hadn't caught any of it.

"I said, do you have any idea who might have wanted to kill her?" he repeated.

"Kill her?" I recited dumbly.

"Detective, maybe we could take this inside?" Drake requested. He slipped his arm around my shoulders and tried to rub some warmth into them.

"Tell you what," Kent said. "I've got some more questions to ask here and I need to take a look outside before these snowy footprints get even more trampled. You guys go back into your own house and I'll come over after awhile and go over this with you."

"Good idea," Drake agreed.

"What about Judy? How's she doing?" I pictured this as just one more thing my fragile neighbor had to cope with.

"We're checking into that." He turned away and Drake steered me toward our front door.

"That was a strange answer, don't you think?" I asked Drake as he opened the front door. The warmth of our living room felt so good, I rubbed my chilled hands together.

"What's going on?" A sleepy Catherine was just emerging from her room, zipping the front of her robe, her hair tousled wildly.

"There's been some problem next door, Mom," Drake said gently. "I think you could go back to bed if you want. The police may be over here after awhile, so we're going to stay up."

"Police? Oh, my god," she exclaimed, instantly more alert. "Well, in that case I'm staying up, too. Let me make us some hot chocolate."

She hurried to the kitchen while I flopped on the sofa. I remembered the jokes Judy and I had made earlier in the day, about bumping off Paula as painfully as possible. God, I hoped she hadn't taken me seriously. I sat with elbows on knees, my face in my hands.

"Hon? You okay?" Drake asked.

I nodded but didn't trust myself to speak. He stuck his index finger under my chin and raised my head until he could see my eyes.

"Sweetheart, *what* is it?"

"What if I had something to do with this?" My throat suddenly felt tight.

"How could you poss—?"

"Judy and I talked about killing Paula," I blurted out.

"Wait . . . what?" Confusion mingled with horror on his face.

"Jokingly! I mean when she came over earlier today—well, I guess it was yesterday now. Anyway, she'd been telling me how Paula was driving her nuts and we got into this little banter about ways to get rid of her. It was just . . . You don't suppose I gave her an idea, do you?"

He put his finger gently on my lips. "Hush now. *No*, you didn't give her any ideas. And no, Judy wouldn't have really hurt Paula. Saying you wish you were rid of someone is *not* the same as killing them."

His voice dropped as Catherine peeked in from the kitchen. "Marshmallows?" she asked.

"Cabinet beside the fridge." I answered in a surprisingly normal tone, but the minute she disappeared my head dropped back into my hands.

"Charlie, take a deep breath," Drake ordered. "Now you're not going to say any of this to Kent Taylor."

"What if I'm concealing evidence?"

"This conversation between you and Judy is not evidence. Not yet, anyway. Just wait to find out what he finds at the . . . the . . ."

"Crime scene," I filled in. "I can't believe this. Our

neighbors' house has become a crime scene."

"Whatever. Just don't impart this particular information to him unless it looks like it really might be relevant. And even then, be very careful what you say."

"Chocolate's ready," Catherine chirped from the doorway. She hipped the swinging door open, her hands loaded with a large tray and three steaming mugs. Drake gave my hand a squeeze, then shoved magazines aside to make space on the coffee table.

We drank our hot chocolate and speculated as to what might be happening next door, with Drake periodically peeking out the front windows to report as various vehicles left. We'd fallen into an almost sleepy silence again when the knock came at the front door at two-thirty. Kent Taylor's appearance and the gust of wintry air he ushered in brought the rest of us around again.

"Do I smell chocolate?" he asked before he'd slipped off his overcoat.

Catherine immediately offered to get him a cup and the rest of us decided we'd take refills too.

He flipped to a new page in his spiral. "Okay, what does

anybody know about the friction between the family next door?"

Nothing like getting straight to the point. I glanced at Drake, a move that I'm sure made it look like I had something to hide.

"Wilbur and Judy appear to get along just great," Drake offered. "Haven't noticed any problems there."

"Well, I'm kind of looking more for information on who might have not been getting along with the victim, Paula Candelaria." Taylor's voice was only a tad short of sarcastic.

"Kent," I began, "I'm not sure there was actually anyone who *did* get along with her." I wrapped my chilly hands around the mug Catherine handed me. "I don't mean to speak ill of the dead," I added hastily, "but Paula was rather—shall we say, abrasive. The kind of person who just rubbed most people the wrong way."

"I'm kind of getting that impression," he admitted. "Okay, I understand there was some kind of altercation over eggnog at some 'do' down at the Country Club?"

I tried to remember back to the cookie swap. It had been a busy week. "Well, there was an incident where Paula broke a glass cup and Chuck Ciacarelli yelled at her. But he's such a grouch, even on a good day. He'd probably yell at Santa for leaving footprints on the roof."

"I heard the exchange went a little beyond that. Ciacarelli carried it on outside and got into quite an argument with the victim and her son after they left the party."

Drake and I looked at each other. "I sure didn't hear anything about that," I offered. "They left before we did, but I never heard any more than what went on in the party room."

Catherine and Drake nodded in agreement.

"Any other incidents you know of?" Taylor asked. "Fights between family members, raised voices, things like that?"

I had a hard time imagining the mild-mannered Wilbur or long-suffering Judy ever having a screaming match with anyone. I shook my head. Judy's complaints about her mother-in-law's behavior were all second hand; I'd never witnessed a nasty exchange between them.

"Who do you think would have a reason to kill Paula?" I asked Kent. "She didn't know anyone here."

"My question exactly. Woman comes to town to visit relatives. Meets a few neighbors. Hard to find someone with motive."

"Was there a break-in? Judy had mentioned that she and Wilbur were invited to a dinner party last night. Did it happen while they were gone?"

"Yeah—they were gone when she died. Supposedly. I'm checking alibis."

An uneasy tremor went through me.

"And what was the cause of death?" Drake asked.

"Looks like a single blow with a fireplace poker. It was lying beside her, bloody, couple of smudgy prints on the handle but it looks like it was wiped down. She was lying in one corner of the couch. Could have been innocently napping or something. The blow caught her in the temple, so it's also possible that she saw her attacker and was standing when she was hit. Could have just fallen in that position."

"There's been a strange car in the neighborhood," Drake mentioned. "Let me get the license number." He headed for the kitchen.

"True," I said. "Paula'd had some bad relationships in the past—ex-husband in California and all. Maybe somebody tracked her down here."

"Yeah, I've got the ex's name," Kent said.

Drake handed him the note with the plate number on it. "New Mexico plate," he said.

"Thanks."

Kent set his mug on the tray and reached for his overcoat. "We'll know more tomorrow."

"Do you plan to do drug or alcohol tests on Paula?" I asked.

He raised an eyebrow.

"Paula drank quite heavily. And from her erratic behavior, I wouldn't be surprised if some drugs were in the mix too." I shrugged. "Just a thought."

"I'm sure they'll look at all that during autopsy."

Drake walked him to the door and Catherine, who'd been yawning for the past half-hour, excused herself to go back to bed. I felt wired. No way would I fall asleep anytime soon.

"I'm going over there," I told Drake.

He started to make some mild protests, but didn't get very far with it. "Okay. I think I'll switch on the bedroom TV for awhile. See you whenever."

I pulled on my down jacket and stepped outside. The air was still, the night black. All the official vehicles had left and the snoopy neighbors had long since tucked back in and turned out their lights. Only our house and the Garfield's showed any sign of activity. Yellow tape still circled their side yard, protecting the patches of snow that hadn't yet melted. I blew out a deep breath, watching the white vapor puff into the darkness, then headed for the front sidewalk. I tapped tentatively on their front door.

"Oh, Charlie!" Wilbur seemed surprised to see me but ushered me in immediately. He wore pale gray pajamas with a tiny pattern on them, topped with a blue and red plaid robe. "Come into the kitchen. I'm trying to get Judy to have some hot chocolate."

His face seemed drawn, with a set of age lines I hadn't noticed before. His eyes were red-rimmed with dark smudges beneath. I followed him into the kitchen. Judy was rummaging through an upper cabinet, her back to the door, her quick movements masking the small whoosh of the swinging door. She was also clad in her nightwear—flannel floor-length gown with flannel ruffles at the cuffs and neck.

"Honey, Charlie's here," Wilbur murmured.

She jumped visibly at the sound of his voice. A mug clattered to the counter top and she automatically reached out to catch it.

"Charlie! Oh, god, I'm glad you're here." She left the mug lying on its side and slumped into a chair at the maple dining table. "I just can't think . . . I mean, I just don't know what . . ." Her fingers fidgeted with the top button of her gown at the base of her throat.

"I know," I said gently. Wilbur patted her on the shoulder as I sat down beside her. "I'm so sorry to hear about what happened."

They both nodded.

"Did the police have any answers for you?"

"Nothing yet," Wilbur volunteered.

"I couldn't keep up with them," Judy added. "I think they went all over the house and spread black powder on everything. I haven't had a chance to check. It's going to be a mess to clean up." She rubbed her index finger around in tiny circles on the table's shiny wood finish.

"Let me get us some hot chocolate," Wilbur offered. "The milk's already hot."

"None for me, thanks. We just drank a couple at home."

He went to the stove and busied himself with the mix and the milk, making two mugs.

"Would it help to tell me about it? Did you come home from your dinner party and just . . . find her?"

"We went over all this so many times with the police," Wilbur said. His voice almost had a sharp edge.

"I'm sorry." I felt like a totally insensitive jerk. "I shouldn't—"

"It's okay," Judy said. "Wilbur, I really don't mind. Investigating is what Charlie does, you know. Maybe she could help."

"Well, I—" I'd told Judy about my brother being a private investigator, and that I was a partner in the firm. I didn't mean to imply that it was really *my* field.

"Yes," she interrupted. "I want to tell you about it and see what you think."

Wilbur picked up his mug and left the room.

"Judy, are you sure this is okay? I mean, well, Wilbur seems upset by my being here."

"You know, I don't really care," she whispered. She took a long swig of her cocoa. "I mean, I do care. I'm sorry Wilbur lost his mother. He's shaken up about it, but I don't think grief has really set in yet. It's just that I really felt like the target of all those police questions earlier, and I don't care whether he wants me to tell you or not. I won't sleep the rest of the night anyway."

"Target? Judy, what do you mean?"

"I guess I'm their main suspect."

Chapter 8

It was no secret that Judy didn't much like her mother-in-law, but to think she would have killed Paula seemed ludicrous. We *were* only kidding around.

"You're not serious—surely."

"Well, let's just say that the questions were going one way when they first got here—what time did we get home, where had we been, was Paula alone when we left, that kind of thing. Then one of the officers who'd been outside came back in the house and there was a little whispered discussion between him and that chubby, bald cop."

Kent Taylor.

"And then the questions started being about my relationship with Paula. Did we ever fight? Did we have words last night? That kind of thing."

Oh, boy. I guess I wasn't the only one Judy'd made little

remarks to.

"Do you want to go over it again?" I asked. "Tell me what happened last night, the sequence of events?"

She drained her cup and shrugged. "Sure." She carried the mug to the sink and ran some water into it.

"Wilbur and I were invited to dinner at the home of some people we know from church. They live off Rio Grande, in that new subdivision west of Old Town."

"Okay."

"We left here at six. Dinner wasn't really ready, so we sat around and talked awhile, drank some iced tea. It was actually refreshing to be around people who don't drink, after the week with Paula's . . . you know.

"So, anyway, we ate about seven-thirty, I'd guess. Then we started a domino game that went on for quite awhile. I developed a horrible headache. I thought it might be a migraine coming on. The game was really in high gear and Wilbur didn't want to leave, so Norma told me to lie down in their guestroom for awhile. I dozed off and must have been in there for an hour or more. But when I woke up the headache was gone."

She'd been pacing the length of the kitchen while she

related all this. Now she sat down again.

"We left their house around eleven, eleven-fifteen. When we walked in the front door, there was Paula, on the sofa." She squeezed her eyes shut like she wanted to erase the picture. "You know, at first I thought she'd passed out there. Her head was on a pillow and one arm and one leg kind of hung over the edge. She was just, you know, sprawled out. Wilbur and I were just talking about whether to wake her up to go to bed when I noticed the blood."

She paused and swallowed.

"Wilbur wanted to revive her. He kept shaking her. I called 911 but she was already . . ."

"It must have been so frightening."

"It was. Charlie, I've only ever seen one dead person, and that was at a funeral home. This was . . . really . . ."

"It's okay. It's over now."

"I just . . . I can't figure out why someone did this."

"Like robbery? Did you check the rest of the house? Maybe they broke in to steal something." Aside from the fact that Paula was a real pain in the neck, I couldn't think of any motives.

"We glanced around a little. We really didn't have much chance. The police were here so quickly. I didn't notice anything missing, though, and they said there was no evidence of a break-in." She glanced nervously at the back door. "I think I'll just check everything one more time. What if we interrupted them when we came home? They might decide to come back."

I went around the house with her and checked all windows and doors. Everything looked secure, and I didn't notice anything major out of place—no missing TV set, no drawers left open with clothing hanging out. Wilbur was locked in the master bath with the shower running, but that was the only window we didn't test. I left a few minutes later, both of us trying to convince the other to sleep well.

I slid into bed beside Drake a few minutes later but didn't actually close my eyes until gray dawn began to show at the windows.

The day after Christmas here in Albuquerque has become nearly the biggest shopping day of the year. Everybody has to rush out to exchange all the stuff they didn't really want for the stuff they could have just bought for themselves if they hadn't spent all their money buying other people stuff *they* really didn't want either. Knowing this, the last places I'd want to be were the malls or downtown. However, curiosity was going to get the best of me and I knew I'd end up in Kent Taylor's office at the main APD downtown station.

I sat in a straight wooden chair across from him, having cruised a four-block area three times to get a parking place. My excuse for coming was that Wilbur and Judy were too upset to ask about the autopsy report and had sent me to do it. My real reason was my usual one—I wanted to know the skinny on what the police were doing.

"Pretty much what we knew at the scene," Kent was saying. "Blow to the head with the fireplace tool. The indent matches the hook on the Garfield's poker. Beyond that, let's see . . blood alcohol level pretty high. Way more than is legal for driving. But then, she wasn't driving, was she? Other drugs— pretty good amount of cocaine. The combination isn't a good one. But she'd probably been mixing them for quite awhile and it wasn't enough to kill her. That's not the full, final report, but it's the important stuff."

"Was there a struggle at the scene?" I hadn't noticed much out of place, but there'd been time to straighten everything by the time I'd arrived last night.

"Not much, if any. Couple of chair cushions on the floor. The son told us he wasn't sure if the front door was locked when they got home."

"How could he not be sure?"

"Said he approached the door, used his key, went on in. Didn't really pay attention to whether the lock was actually engaged or not."

"So, Paula could have opened the door to her killer?"

"Or it could have been someone with a key."

"Who else would have a key but Wilbur or Judy?"

"Exactly. That, coupled with a few other things are pointing to her as the main suspect."

"Really, Kent. Judy?"

He ticked off points on his fingers. "One, she made no secret of it that she wouldn't mind seeing her mother-in-law dead. Two, she disappeared from the dinner party she was at for—let's see, the hostess told us--well over an hour. Three, there were more sets of tire tracks in the snow at the front of their driveway than they can account for. Said they went out twice all day; there are three sets of tracks."

"All those tracks are from their car? For sure?"

"Looks that way. And, four, the only prints on the weapon belong to your neighbor, Judy."

"Well, whoever used it obviously either wore gloves or wiped it clean. Of course, there would be some partial prints of Judy's. The poker's in her home."

His look told me I was getting a little too argumentative.

"Okay, okay, I'll shut up. But are you at least looking for other suspects too? Kent, I can't believe this quiet, mild-mannered woman is a killer. She just isn't the type."

"She's pregnant, you know. Hormones and all."

"Kent! Oh, please!"

"Hey, I'm just saying there's a case right now where this woman's using raging hormones as a defense. Doesn't deny she did the crime." He shrugged and gave me a raised eyebrow.

I gritted my teeth and suggested I better get going. He didn't contradict me.

Outside, the sky was a clear, pale blue and the wind was sharp. I pulled on my knitted mittens and zipped my parka up to my chin. I race-walked around the block to dissipate a little energy. Back at the car, I fumbled with the key twice before getting the door open.

We'd be lucky if she killed herself. Hadn't Judy grumbled those very words to me at the cookie swap?

I could just kill her. Didn't she once say that to me, too? She must have said it to other neighbors too, because the police had obviously gotten some pretty strong ammunition in their queries among the crowd last night.

This wasn't looking good. I didn't have any idea how long it would take Kent to put together enough evidence to arrest her, but that sure looked like the track he was taking.

Chapter 9

I cranked the Jeep's engine to life and cruised the downtown streets before turning west on Central. Although we weren't officially open all this week, on an impulse I decided to stop at the office before heading home.

The gray and white Victorian sits in a neighborhood that's partly commercial and partly residential, and has been that way for many years. We like being on the quiet side street and the fact that there are some full-time neighbors around who keep an eye on the place. I pulled my Jeep into the driveway that follows the left hand side of the property to the back, where a one-time carriage house serves as storage and the yard as parking area.

The old house was cool and echoey, lonely feeling in its holiday abandonment. The linoleum on the kitchen floor creaked as I walked across it, switching on lights, heading for the hallway to turn up the thermostat. A pile of mail sprawled on the floor inside the front door and I scooped it up and deposited it on Sally's desk. Absently, I picked up each piece and sorted them into piles—for Sally, Ron and myself. I'd become so engrossed in the mindless flipping of envelopes that I nearly jumped out of my skin when the phone rang.

Patting myself on the chest, I let it go four times so the answering machine would pick up.

"Charlie, are you there?" Drake's voice came through the tinny little speaker.

I reached for Sally's handset. "I'm here. How did you know?"

"Just a wild guess. I tried your cell, but it's turned off. So I took a chance that you'd stopped at the office."

I reached into my purse as he spoke and checked my little phone. The battery had gone dead sometime in the past few days.

". . . taking her away right now," he was saying.

"What? I missed the first part of that."

"The police have just taken Judy Garfield."

A ball of lead settled in my stomach. "Damn that Kent Taylor," I railed. "I just saw him and he knew this was happening. Didn't say a word about it to me."

"Wilbur's over here now, out in the kitchen with Mom. He doesn't know what to do next."

"Has he called a lawyer?"

"I don't think so. They don't know many people here. Can you recommend anyone?"

"Let me put you on hold. I'll check Ron's Rolodex." I pressed the red button and trotted up the stairs.

Ron's office is on the left, with mine across the hall. His desk, as usual, was a hodgepodge of paper—piles of unopened mail mixed in with telephone messages and sheets from yellow lined pads. I'll never know how the man finds anything in here. I patted down the mountain of stuff until I felt a hard, square shape resembling the Rolodex.

Cradling the phone to my shoulder and stabbing the button for line one, I assured myself that Drake was still on the line.

"Hold on a second while I try to remember Ron's filing system," I said. "He doesn't do anything the way anyone else does." On a lucky guess, I flipped to the letter L and discovered several cards with Lawyer written at the top. I thumbed through them to see if I recognized any names.

"Might try Martin Palmer or George Collins," I suggested, reading off the phone numbers. "Or if Judy would feel more comfortable with a woman, I've heard Natalie Rice is good. Don't know if any of them will be in their offices the day after Christmas, but maybe there'll be a message with an alternate way to contact them."

I closed the Rolodex lid. "Did they actually arrest Judy, or just take her down for questioning?" I asked. I listened while Drake repeated the question to Wilbur.

"He's not really sure. They didn't put cuffs on her."

"Well, either way, she probably should have an attorney with her. I'll get off the phone so you guys can make some calls. There's not much to do here, so I should be home soon."

I switched off Ron's light, went back downstairs, and finished stacking the mail. After carrying mine and Ron's upstairs to our respective offices, I scanned the empty rooms to be sure everything was in place, debating the wisdom of driving back downtown to see if I could help Judy. Decided they probably wouldn't let me see her, since I wasn't legal counsel. I locked the back door and headed home.

Wilbur, Drake, and Catherine were sitting around the kitchen table when I arrived.

"Any news?" I asked.

"We reached Martin Palmer on his cell phone," Drake said. "He's on his way to APD to see if he can straighten this out."

Wilbur looked more helpless than ever, clutching an empty mug in his hands and staring at a spot somewhere in the middle of the table. His thin, sandy hair stood out in tufts on the sides, as if he'd been running his hands through it repeatedly. Catherine looked up at me with a raised eyebrow, which I took to mean that things didn't look too great.

"Would anyone like a sandwich?" I offered, needing something to do besides stand around.

Catherine jumped up and headed toward the refrigerator. "Yes, that's a great idea. Let's put some lunch together for everyone."

The phone rang just as I was reaching into the breadbox. We all froze in place. Drake reached for it on the second ring.

"Martin Palmer," he said, handing the receiver over to Wilbur, whose hand shook visibly when he took it.

"Uh-huh, uh-huh." He nodded his head as the attorney

talked. "Is that it then? Uh-huh." He pressed the button to end the call and set the phone on the table.

We all stood in our frozen positions while he scrubbed at the sides of his hair some more.

"Well?" Drake finally asked in a remarkably calm voice. I wanted to scream.

Wilbur let out a huge sigh. "They've charged her." His voice nearly broke and he swallowed deeply. His Adam's apple traveled up and down again before more words came out. "She has to stay there until a hearing tomorrow. The judge will decide whether she can be out on bail."

Catherine crossed to him and put her arm around his thin shoulders.

"Surely she'll be granted bail," I pressed. "She's certainly not a flight risk or a danger to society." I pulled slices of bread out of the loaf and began smearing them with mayonnaise.

"I can't believe this is happening at all," Drake argued.

That pretty well summed it up for all of us.

"Let me call Ron this afternoon," I said. "Maybe we can do a little investigating of our own and get some leads on the real killer."

"You know the police aren't going to take kindly to our interference in an active investigation," Ron told me when I finally reached him about four o'clock.

"Is it really an active investigation?" I asked. "They've got a suspect and they're about to indict her tomorrow. I seriously doubt they're pushing real hard to find any other suspects."

He grumbled a bit but basically agreed. "So, what other leads do you have?"

I had to admit there really weren't any, other than my firm belief that Judy just didn't have what it took to swing a poker at someone and bash them in the head with it. "I'm going to see what I can find out from Wilbur. And maybe from the other neighbors Paula talked to. Maybe somebody can give us some insight. Right now, her life is pretty much a mystery."

Drake had done a good job of distracting Wilbur from his problems for the afternoon. The two men had cleaned up the remains of the luminarias from both our yards and were raking a few of autumn's leftover leaves from our backyard. I donned a light jacket and went out long enough to suggest that I'd warm up the leftover green chile stew and that Wilbur should stay for dinner. In the meantime, would he mind if I took a peek through Paula's things in their guestroom? My own guess, privately, was that the police would have removed anything of use, but there was no harm in looking for clues.

The Garfield house felt like a place that's been suddenly abandoned. There were dishes on the dining table, where Judy and Wilbur had been having breakfast when the police arrived. I carried them to the kitchen and ran some warm water over them in the sink, put away the butter, and wiped off the countertops. Turned on a couple of lamps against the late afternoon twilight.

Their floor plan was similar to ours, three bedrooms off a hall on the north side of the house. It only took a minute to figure out which one Paula'd used. The rumpled bed had probably remained unmade during her entire visit, I guessed. The disarray of the comforter and blankets was complete. The tight red dress she'd worn to the cookie swap lay draped over a chair back, with her outfit from Christmas Eve piled on top of it. A suitcase was on the floor against one wall, the lid open and lacy underthings spilling over the sides. The bag had been thoroughly rummaged, whether by the police or by Paula herself, I couldn't tell. Of course, the other possibility was that the killer might have searched her room for something. What that might be, or whether he'd found it, was anyone's guess.

Knowing that I was probably just repeating someone else's moves, I ran my hands through the suitcase, but nothing incriminating jumped out at me. I took the time to pull each item out, give it a look, and fold it neatly, making a little stack on the floor beside me. Two pair of jeans, three sweaters, an assortment of dainties—not much else. A tote bag, the kind made of canvas with handles of webbing, stood beside the suitcase and was crammed with shoes. I pulled them out—pink tennies, black pumps, black boots, silver flats—shaking each upside down in case any notes written in invisible ink or keys to bus depot lockers might fall out. No such luck.

Tentatively, in case something sharp reached out at me, I felt around the inside of the tote. It was exactly what it appeared to be, medium weight canvas with no hidden compartments. The suitcase was another story. It was one of those ubiquitous black airline bags with wheels and a pull-out handle. Under the flimsy plastic lining, I felt the mechanism for the wheels. One side had just a touch more padding than the other and my curious fingers poked around, exploring that oddity, until I discovered a narrow slit in the lining.

With thumb and forefinger, I reached inside and came out with the corner of a zipper-type sandwich bag. A tug at the bag brought the whole thing out and I saw, not especially to my surprise, that it contained white powder. Now I know these things are usually referred to in grams or kilos or such, but that was completely outside my realm. I'd put the contents at about a tablespoon or two.

Probably the cocaine that had been found in her system. I wasn't about to dip my finger into it and take a taste. How was I going to know what it would taste like anyway?

I placed the small bag on the floor and proceeded with my search of the room. The nightstand drawer yielded a paperback romance and a pair of reading glasses that I'd bet Paula never wore in front of anyone else. The adjoining bathroom vanity held a large makeup case with a mirror encircled by a row of Hollywood-style makeup lights. Everything in the case looked standard for a woman who took great pains with her face and hair. No more little baggies. And if there had been, I was sure the police had thoroughly checked over this treasure trove and removed anything of use to them. I wasn't interested so much in her stash as I was in where she'd gotten it.

Since it looked as if Paula was crazy enough to travel with her powdered treasure hidden away in her airline bag, did that mean she'd brought it all with her? Or did she have a connection here in town? For a person who planned to move in and stay awhile, I couldn't imagine the tiny bit I'd found would last very long. And based on the behavior I'd witnessed the couple of times I'd been around her, she'd probably already dipped into it more than once.

I stood in the doorway between bedroom and bath, pondering what I might have missed.

A purse.

Every woman carried a purse and it would surely be where she kept those items she'd want close at hand. An address book, photos, stuff like that. I crossed the bedroom again and pulled open the dresser drawers. The top two were empty, the next two held spare linens and towels—obviously things that belonged to the household, not to Paula. The bottom drawer was where I hit paydirt. Under another stack of towels, was a black handbag, not Paula's large everyday one, but a small quilted leather one about six by twelve inches, with a gold chain

for a strap. Small and dressy enough that it could double as
an evening bag, but large enough to carry the essentials. And
inside, I found two very essential items: an address book and a
wallet with a nice juicy section of photos. Why the police hadn't
seen fit to take these, I didn't know, but I wasn't passing up a
chance like this.

A quick glance told me that none of the names or faces—
except one stiffly posed photo of Wilbur and Judy—meant
anything to me. But maybe Wilbur could identify more of them
and give me a whole load of clues.

I realized that it was completely dark outside now and
since I'd volunteered to provide dinner for everyone, it was
time I hustled myself back home. I'd just closed the drapes in
the guest room and switched off the light, pulling the door
closed behind me when I bumped into Wilbur in the hallway.

Chapter 10

O
h! I didn't hear you out here," I gasped.

"Um, I just thought I better check on you. See how things were coming along." He fumbled with a ring full of keys.

"You're coming back to our place for dinner, aren't you?" I sidestepped him and worked my way toward the living room. "I found a couple of items you might be able to help with—if that's okay." I held up the wallet and address book.

"Sure. Drake told me to come right back. I just thought I'd be sure the house was locked and some lights were left on. That's what Judy . . ." He glanced around uncertainly.

"Okay, then, let's go." I took his elbow and steered him toward the door. He gave one sharp glance toward the sofa where his mother had died, then followed me timidly.

I switched on the porch light and twisted the little thing in the middle of the doorknob to lock it. I made a show of checking it after I closed it behind us.

"All set?" I asked.

Wilbur nodded absently and followed me across the lawn to our front porch. I wasn't sure how much help he'd be when we started going through Paula's possessions. He was clearly still dazed by the dual shock of his mother's murder and his wife's being arrested for it.

Inside, the house exuded the warm fragrance of meaty chile stew and Catherine had warmed some garlic bread to go with it. We served everything at the kitchen table and the four of us sat down. Despite his glazed appearance, Wilbur put away two bowls of stew and perked up somewhat afterward. Drake and Catherine cleared the dishes and put coffee on while I pulled my chair closer to Wilbur's and brought out Paula's things.

"I could use your help now, Wilbur. Can you identify the people in these photos?"

He pushed his glasses farther up his nose and opened the wallet. His gaze caught for a moment on Paula's driver's license before he flipped to the photo section. The first was of a dark-haired man, probably Hispanic.

"That's Ray. The fifth."

"The recent ex?"

He nodded. "I'm not even really sure the divorce was final. She may have just left him when she showed up here."

"Really? I was under the impression that they'd been apart for awhile." Something came back to me. Paula had said the past year had been hard because of the divorce. I thought she meant it had dragged on that long.

"No, I don't think so," Wilbur said when I mentioned it. "The split was pretty new. But, who knows? Mother sometimes came up with a variety of stories to suit her purposes."

It was the first time, I realized, that I'd heard Wilbur say anything negative about his mother.

"Now this picture? These are my brother's two girls."

"I didn't realize you had a brother."

"An older half-brother, actually. He's from her first marriage. I was from the second. After that, I think she dropped the idea that men would be permanent in her life. At least she didn't bother to have any more kids with the others."

"Were they close? Your mother and half-brother?"

He made a snorting sound. "Not at all. Amos wrote her

off when the second marriage failed. He's a very traditional kind of guy."

And you're not? I clamped my lips together, hoping I hadn't actually voiced this aloud.

He was quiet for a moment, then seemed to realize he still had the wallet in his hand.

"This picture of his girls must be at least ten or twelve years old. These little kids in pigtails are now in high school. Doing really well, too. Judy and I get them birthday and Christmas gifts every year. Used to spend the holidays with them when we were all in the Chicago area."

"Back to Ray," I said. "I'm thinking any clues that will be useful to Judy are going to be more recent. Did Paula tell me she and Ray lived in California? Is he still there?"

"Guess so. I have to admit, I followed my brother's lead in not getting too close to Mother's husbands. It just didn't pay." He was flipping idly through the photos. "Come to think of it, though, she had a phone call from him right after she got here. Could the phone company tell you where it came from?"

"Probably." If the police hadn't already checked this lead, they should have. Maybe Ron could pull some strings if the police wouldn't cooperate.

Catherine brought Wilbur a cup of tea, coffee for me.

"In fact, when she first got on the line with Ray, I think Mother asked him something about how the weather was out in sunny old L.A."

I'd pulled a notepad out of the kitchen drawer and made myself a note to find a number for Ray Candelaria.

"Was their divorce bitter?" I asked.

"I got the feeling it was. Like I said, I tuned out a lot of it. I know Mother wasn't happy with him for a long time. She hinted, but never really said, that he abused her. Of course, all that only came out after she'd left him. I overheard her telling Judy about an incident where Ray threatened her if she left, but she said she wasn't taking any sh--, well, any bad stuff from him. She left anyway."

"Wilbur! Don't you see that this could be the whole story right there? Maybe Ray decided to make good on his threat. Maybe he couldn't stand her being gone, holidays and all, and he came after her." I felt myself getting excited that another suspect was turning up so quickly.

He looked skeptical. "Ray? Um, I don't know."

Was Wilbur just one of those gentle types who didn't truly believe that a man would harm a woman? I decided I might have to set him straight on that someday.

He was pointing to another of the photos. "That was my dad," he said. "Too bad he died before he got to see our baby." His voice cracked slightly on the last word and he looked at me with sorrow in his gray eyes. "What will happen if Judy—"

"Let's deal with one thing at a time," I told him. "I'm sure we're going to find out who really did this long before it's time for the baby to come."

I sure hoped we would anyway. We spent a few more minutes going through the address book, a cheap thing in a vinyl cover. Paula had even filled out the few lines inside the front cover with "This book belongs to:" information. At least I had her previous address and phone number in California now.

Wilbur didn't recognize most of the names in the book. He'd pointed out a couple of cousins from the Midwest, but didn't know any of her friends from her years in California. He let me take the picture of Ray Candelaria from the wallet and said I could keep the address book as long as I needed it. He was beginning to look faded again by the time he went back

home.

Chapter 11

I spent a restless night pondering my next moves. I wanted to question Ray Candelaria and didn't think I'd learn what I needed to know over the phone. A trip to Los Angeles might be in order, but I wasn't sure I should just do it. Wilbur hadn't actually hired us to investigate his mother's death. As the accountant for our firm, I knew we were flush enough for the year that a plane ticket to L.A. and a night or two in a hotel wouldn't break us. We could consider it pro bono, but I wasn't sure how Ron would feel about that. The only conclusion I'd reached by two-thirty a.m. was that I would run it past him at a more decent hour.

Catherine was already up when I went into the kitchen. The smell of coffee pulled at me. I let the dogs out into the back yard and poured myself a cup, then sat at the table with her. Once again, I felt so thankful that my mother-in-law and I had a good relationship.

"So, what do you think?" she asked, fingering the address book.

"Not much idea yet. But I need to talk to Ray Candelaria. I think he'll know something."

"There's another name in this book I'd check if I were you," she suggested. "I think he might have sold Paula drugs."

"You know which one it is?"

"Gus," Catherine said. "Paula just dropped this on me that day we went shopping. It was so casual I almost didn't notice. She said something like, 'Guess I'll have to find me a Gus here.' I was driving and I guess something pulled my attention away and I never did ask anything about this Gus. But later, when we stopped for lunch, she excused herself to go to the ladies room and when she came back she seemed much more energetic. And her nose was kind of red. I thought, coke. She's doing coke. But what was I going to do? I couldn't ditch her at the mall. I just tried to get her home as quickly as possible."

"You never mentioned any of this! Was she, like, out of control or anything?"

"Oh, no. It startled me at first, realizing it, but later I thought no, that's just what Paula's like. Not somebody I'd want as a friend, obviously, but I didn't think it was up to me to preach to her either."

We'd both finished our coffee and I got up to refill the mugs. "I think I'll go into the office today, check some of this stuff with Ron, maybe do a little more investigating. Want a piece of toast or something first?" I had let Catherine fend for herself for much of her visit, and now I was offering nothing more than toast for breakfast.

"That's okay, Charlie. You go ahead and get ready for work. I can make something later."

Thirty minutes later, I'd had a quick shower, an even quicker kiss from my hubby, and was on my way to the office. Ron had told me Christmas Day that he didn't plan to take the whole week off and would probably spend part of the weekend catching up on paperwork. His car was already there when I arrived.

The kitchen smelled of burnt coffee, which is usually an indicator that Ron has made a pot of his killer-strong brew and let some of it dribble onto the hot metal plate on the coffee maker. Having tasted this stuff in the past, I opted to make myself a cup of tea in the microwave.

"Anybody home?" I called as I climbed the stairs.

His voice came trailing from his office in a monotone. Phone conversation. I flipped on the light in my own office and realized that the pile of mail from the previous day hadn't magically disappeared. I sat down to sort through it.

"Thought you weren't coming in this week," Ron said.

I hadn't heard him approach and I nearly sloshed my tea. Recovering, I set the mug down on a coaster and shoved the mail aside.

"I didn't think so either, but this situation with the neighbors has kinda taken over my time for the past couple of days. Wilbur is really devastated. He can hardly answer a question coherently."

"Well, who wouldn't be? The papers are full of it. Having his mother murdered, then his wife accused of the crime. What a mess."

"Pregnant wife. Did I tell you that?" I drained my mug. "Anyway, I've come up with a couple of clues."

He grinned with a knowing little twist to his mouth. "Couldn't resist, could you?"

"Well . . ."

"So, are we hired, or what?"

"That hasn't come up. Like I said, Wilbur's a wreck. And I don't know how much money they have."

"So ask a few questions. We can do a charitable deed now and then," he said.

"Would the charity include my making a quick trip to L.A.?"

He rolled his eyes and puffed out a big sigh, but he didn't say no. An hour later I'd made reservations for the 4:10 flight on Southwest and a room downtown. I rushed through some routine paperwork and gathered my notes before dashing home to pack and spend a little time with the family before leaving.

By 5:10 I was airborne, somewhere over Arizona. Glass of wine in hand, I was transferring names and addresses to my little spiral notebook and pinpointing places on my roadmap of the greater Los Angeles area, which was certainly greater in scope than anything I usually dealt with. By the time I picked up my rental car and headed into the maze of freeways, it was dark and the commuting drivers were even surlier than I. I was beginning to question the wisdom of the whole trip.

My research and mapping had indicated that Ray

Candelaria's place was between the airport and my hotel, so it
only made sense to stop there first. I exited and pulled out my
map at the first stoplight. I happened to glance up and realized
wasn't in a great neighborhood and that reading my roadmap
at the intersection definitely branded me as an out-of-towner. I
laid the map down and locked my doors.

At the next well-lighted place, a 24-hour medical clinic, I
pulled in and parked under a lamppost. Getting my bearings,
discovered I was only six blocks from my goal. Ray's home
turned out to be a white-stuccoed, red-tile roofed, mission
tyled home in a decent neighborhood. The lawn was well-
groomed and elegant palms flanked the sidewalk leading up
from the street. There were no cars in the driveway, but lights
shone from inside the house. I pressed the doorbell and set off
a short symphony.

A woman in her thirties, with long, dark hair and twelve
ounces of mascara opened the door. She wore a red and gold
caftan and strappy gold sandals. One hand held a martini glass
and the other stayed firmly on the doorsill.

"Is Ray Candelaria home?" I asked.

She appraised me slowly, top to toe. When she'd decided

that a travel-worn, woman with hair in a ponytail, wearing jeans with scuffed knees, a faded turtleneck, and dingy Nikes wasn't a threat to her, she stepped aside.

"What was your name?" she asked, finally figuring out that she might have admitted a census taker or insurance salesperson.

I handed her my business card from RJP Investigations.

"Charlie? What kind of a name is that for a woman?"

I slipped on a tight smile. I really didn't want to go into the whole explanation of how I'd been named for two maiden aunts and that Charlotte Louise had never quite stuck to me. When I didn't answer, she turned on her heel and headed upstairs. I waited until she'd disappeared, then looked around.

The entryway was small, and opened directly on the living room. Beyond that I could see the L of a dining room, with a kitchen and breakfast area directly in front of me. Everything was done in shades of blue and cream. I stepped into the living room and examined a group of photos standing in brass frames on a bookcase. There were plenty of Ray, some including the woman who'd opened the door. None including Paula.

Considering their divorce was only recently final, he'd done a remarkable job of mopping up traces of her and installing her replacement quickly enough.

Voices from upstairs caught my attention. The male sounded grumbly and included something along the lines of, '. . . and you let her in?" Almost immediately, a door closed firmly and the woman appeared at the top of the stairs. Putting on a weak smile, she tottered down on her slender heels and approached me.

"What did you say this was about?" she asked.

"I didn't." I gave her a minute to come up with something, but she wasn't ready with anything quick. "It's something I have to discuss with Ray."

I walked over to a very straight wingback chair and sat down.

"He's getting dressed. It'll be a few minutes."

"That's fine." I guess I looked prepared to camp there because she didn't say anything else. She went into the kitchen and rattled some ice cubes in a glass.

A good ten minutes passed, during which the woman disappeared into another room beyond the kitchen. Sounds of doors opening and closing and the occasional running water upstairs told me that Ray was making no haste with his toilette. I walked back over to the bookcase and continued my perusal.

Unfortunately, the reading material was limited to romance novels and a few volumes on how to improve your golf game. There were no scrapbooks or albums or other juicy stuff. The furniture was the mid-priced kind you found at outlet places and the art on the walls was of the starving artist variety. I was about to start toe-tapping when I noticed Ray at the top of the stairs. I wondered if he'd been standing there watching me give the place the once-over.

"Ray Candelaria?" I walked toward him and extended my hand as he reached the bottom step. He was in his mid forties, probably ten years younger than Paula, or more. Black hair, razor cut to perfection, tailored gray slacks and a pink polo shirt, about two too many gold chains.

He held up my card and looked at it. "You're an investigator from Albuquerque?"

"That's right. Could we sit down a minute?"

He ushered me back into the living room and we took chairs at opposite ends of a crushed velvet sofa.

"Have you heard about Paula?" I began tentatively.

His expression said 'the bitch,' although the words didn't come out. "What about her?"

"That she was killed a couple of days ago?"

His surprise seemed genuine. His face screwed up in puzzlement. "Killed? What happened?"

So the Albuquerque police hadn't considered Ray worth talking to.

"It was murder." I didn't know any other way to say it and still get to the point quickly. "She was visiting her son and daughter-in-law at the time."

"The one in Albuquerque."

"Yes."

"Think I met that one a couple of times," he said. "You know, Paula and I were only together a couple years. Fun while we were just fooling around, you know. Sailing up the coast, doing the sights, hanging out in some good clubs. But then we got married. Thing she had about 'commitment.' I don't know. The fun just kind of went out of it after that."

He shrugged and reached toward the coffee table, picking up a small wooden box with a hinged lid. He began flipping the lid open and shut, clicking it repeatedly.

"When did you see her last?"

"Oh, gosh—" he glanced upward "—way before the divorce actually went through. Probably been a couple months anyway. Maybe more than that."

"What was she doing during that time? I mean before she showed up at Wilbur's house."

"My guess? I mean, I don't really *know*. My guess is, hanging out in some flophouse." He snapped the box's lid loudly and set it back on the coffee table. Thank goodness—I'd been about ready to snatch it away from him.

He rubbed his hands through his hair and it fell perfectly back into place. His gaze met mine firmly. "Paula couldn't give up the drugs. I mean, heck, I'll smoke a little dope now and then, do a little coke at a party or something. But for Paula that was just the appetizer. She'd started with crack a few months before I finally told her to get out. Who knows what else she's tried by now."

"Who supplied her? Was there some guy named Gus?"

His mouth twisted into a grimace. "Oh yeah. Gus."

I waited silently, sure that there was more to come.

"Met Gus at a party at my boss's house in Brentwood. We both did."

"Nice neighborhood. What kind of business?"

"Timeshares. Sales have been good the last few years. I'm doing okay." I remembered a sales brochure I'd come across, tucked between two of the golf books.

"What about this Gus?"

He snorted. "The guy is slime. I have *no* idea how he got into this party, must have been on the arm of somebody connected. Paula gravitated right to him. Don't know how, but those types always find each other. I had to drag her out of the kitchen to go home. But they stayed in touch—I know they did."

"Any idea where he lives?" I'd found a phone number in Paula's address book, but nothing more.

He shook his head. "She probably never went there anyway. Probably just met him places."

"Know where he hangs out?"

He gave me the names of a couple of clubs and I wrote them down in my notebook. The tinkling of ice cubes reminded me of the other woman in the house. I hadn't seen her cross the foyer. How long had she been listening in the kitchen?

Chapter 12

It was completely dark when I emerged from Ray's house and I thought how odd it looked to see Christmas lights on palm trees and flowering shrubs. I spent a couple of minutes in the car studying the map to figure out where I was going next. One of the clubs was near my hotel, so I decided to check in and freshen up first. The real action probably didn't start until later anyway.

My room was on the sixth floor, giving me a swell view of the windows of an office building across the street. A surprising number were lit, considering it was Friday night. I took a quick shower and browsed my suitcase to see what I'd brought that might be appropriate for night life. Nothing, really

I settled on a newer pair of jeans--ones without the knees worn white—and a white tank top. I'd brought it along thinking the California climate might be a lot warmer than ours although it wasn't exactly tank weather. With a denim jacket, I might pass. I rummaged through my sparse makeup bag and found a pair of rhinestone earrings that had probably been in there for years. I could probably rinse the face powder off them. I looked at the ensemble spread out on the bed and really just wished I could put on my flannel jammies and watch TV before falling asleep early.

After a quick call to Drake to let him know I'd made the trip okay, I decided I better keep moving while my momentum was up. I got dressed, put on way more makeup than I usually do, and fluffed my hair to double its volume. Surveying the result in the mirror, I decided I would just avoid mirrors the rest of the evening.

The first club, known simply as Billy's, turned out to be in a not too bad neighborhood, luckily, since I had to park three blocks away. I carefully locked the rental car and clutched my purse against me, wishing I'd been able to bring my new pistol with me. These kinds of situations make me extremely edgy.

I used the three block walk to work up a little hip shake and throw on some attitude. By the time I approached Billy's, I was ready for anything. It was one of those places where people line up outside for their turn to get in and a seven-foot-tall black guy with a shaved head and three gold earrings guards the entry. I could see that I'd never make the cut without a story. I strutted right up to him.

"Hi, I'm supposed to meet Gus here," I said, craning my neck to look him in the eye.

"Oh yeah?" His eyes traveled down to the dip in the front of my tank top. I forced myself not to reach up and close the gap.

"Yeah." I hoped I managed to make it sound saucy. "I'm a friend of Paula's."

Something shifted in his face. "Hold on. Let me check." He gripped the shoulder of a younger, shorter, white guy and whispered something to him. The young one disappeared inside.

"Wait right here," the guard said in a deep baritone.

He turned to the next couple standing in the line. I felt like I didn't quite know what to do with my hands. I moved a little to the beat of the music coming from inside and hoped I didn't look totally nerdy. Stares from the other people in line were beginning to become noticeable but I refused to meet their gazes or apologize for skipping to the front.

It took about five minutes for the runner to come back. Apparently I'd been given the go-ahead. Interesting. Paula must have been a good customer. The huge guy moved the padded rope barrier aside and ushered me through. I didn't know where to find Gus, or what he looked like, but figured this wasn't the moment to ask.

I walked into the assault of deafening music, strobing lights, clouds of cigarette smoke, and writhing bodies. I stood to the side for a minute, adjusting to it all, before making my way to the bar. I ordered a beer, which I usually don't drink, figuring that would make it easy for me to nurse one drink for quite awhile and create no danger that I'd be too intoxicated to drive.

While the bartender drew it into a tall mug, I scanned the room. On the far side, a row of booths lined the wall, most of them filled with couples. One corner booth was occupied by a stringy looking white guy, flanked by two girls, one black and one white. Two other men sat on either side of the girls. They were getting with the music and clearly enjoying themselves. The white guy in the middle was more intent. Gus.

I confirmed it with the bartender as I paid for my beer.

Hiking my purse strap firmly onto my shoulder, I readopted my attitude, picked up my beer, and headed his way. I hadn't yet decided on my approach, so I strolled between tables and dancers, smiling vacantly, pretending to really get into the scene. By the time I'd reached the row of booths, I noticed that Gus was eyeing me. I caught the stare and gave it right back.

"Yeah?" His voice was surly. His gaunt face showed a couple days worth of stubble, and his streaky blond hair looked like it hadn't been washed in a week. The black girl had her arm draped over the back of the booth behind him.

"Paula said I should come see you." I stood with my weight on one hip, going for a casual attitude.

His eyes narrowed. "Yeah. So?"

"She said you got some really good—" I hoped my eyebrows conveyed the message, since I didn't know the slang word for it.

"You ain't from around here," he said.

"Nah. Met her in New Mexico. Happened to be here on, let's say, business. Just lookin' for something to make the trip a little more enjoyable."

He turned toward the guy closest to me who was sitting in

he end seat of the booth. "Clear out."

The man grabbed the hand of the white girl. "C'mon, let's
dance."

They slid out of the booth and Gus gestured for me to
take the empty seat. I did, staying within jumping distance of
the opening.

"Whatta ya want?" he asked. Getting right down to
business.

I shrugged. "Just a little grass, I guess. What'll twenty
bucks get me?"

"That's *it*?"

"I'm only in town till tomorrow. Don't want to get caught
with it on the airplane."

"So, going back to New Mexico?"

"Yeah. Back to the grind." I slid a folded twenty across the
table toward him. He took a pinch from a zipper bag, put it in
an empty one, and slid the little bag to me. "I'll give Paula your
regards."

Something in his face changed. "What're you up to?" His
eyes had become slits.

I glanced around the table. The other two had suddenly

taken an interest in me too. "What do you mean, what am I up to?" I tried to dish it right back at him, but wasn't feeling overly confident at the moment.

"Paula's dead." He watched closely for my reaction.

"What! No way, man. I just saw her last week. She looked great." I shook my head back and forth. "No way could she be dead."

Apparently my feigned shock convinced him. He shrugged. "You'll see."

"Well . . . what happened? How'd you find out?"

"Let's just say a mutual friend told me. We got a short grapevine here."

The black girl forced a laugh and nodded agreement. I took a long pull on my beer to give myself a moment to decide how to handle this. When the chuckles died down I shrugged.

"So, what? Accident, or something?"

"Yeah, let's just say she accidentally forgot to pay her bills." He grinned for the first time. The man really should invest in some good dental work.

"Too bad." I gave a couldn't-give-a-shit shrug. "Well, it's been real."

I stood up and tucked my little purchase into my purse. Resisting the urge to look back at the table, I sauntered toward the ladies room at the back of the club. It looked like I had the place to myself. I took one of the three stalls and slid the latch, blowing out a deep pent-up breath. I did a quick pee, dropped the baggie of pot in after, and flushed. At the row of sinks, I stopped to wash my hands, knowing that I'd want another shower back in my room before I could go to sleep.

"All right, bitch, the truth!" A hand grabbed me from behind, long nails digging into my bicep.

I whirled around to find the black girl from the table. She shoved me against the wall, the electric hand dryer jamming into the small of my back. Pain shot down both legs and I struck out, whipping my arm free at the same time I rammed the heel of my hand into her chest. Her butt hit a sink and it rattled slightly, like it might come off the wall.

"Slow down a second," I yelled before she could come at me again.

She braced herself against the sink, while I backed up to a flat place on the wall.

"What makes you think I'm 'up to something'? What's with

all this third degree stuff from Gus, anyway?" I snarled the words, not faking the anger.

"You—prissy little white girl—come in here with that story about Paula sending you. Paula'd never be friends with somebody like you."

My mind whirled, searching for a way to handle this. "Okay." I slumped against the wall. "Okay, look, you're right. Paula and I weren't exactly friends."

She leaned back against the sink, crossing her arms under her ample breasts.

"Look," I said, "I know Paula was murdered. Okay, I wasn't surprised when Gus told me."

She tapped an index finger against her upper arm.

"It's just that a friend is accused of killing her, and this lady, well, there's just no way she's got it in her to kill anybody. So I'm just asking around, trying to figure out what really happened."

"And you think Gus got somethin' to do with it?"

"You don't?"

"I *know* he don't. Gus been here, in this club, at that table, every night for the whole two years I known him. Gus, he may be sorta messed up. I mean, a dealer, he shouldn't be *doin'* the stuff, you know. He make some money if he jus' sell it. Gus, he dumb enough to use it too." She uncrossed her arms and propped herself against the sink's edge, staring at the floor. "It's us' . . . he's my man. I don't know how to make him quit." Her voice cracked a little.

"Okay, look, I'll take your word for it. He does look like a fixture here."

"Damn straight. B'lieve it or not, Gus ain't gonna get so worked up over a piece of junkie like that Paula Candelaria. What'd be his reason to kill her? Why'd he even care?"

"Cause she didn't pay her bills?" I ventured.

"Yeah, like she gonna pay 'em now?"

Good point. I stood up and retrieved my purse from where it had landed beside a trash can. She grabbed my arm again, more gently this time.

"He's just a lotta talk. Leave him alone, okay?"

"Okay. Look, I'm not the law or anything. I can't actually do anything to him."

She backed away and let me pass. As I walked out the door, he was checking her makeup in the mirror.

Chapter 13

I felt like I was batting zero when I got on the plane the next day, heading back to Albuquerque. I'd left the club last night at a leisurely pace, casually inquiring of both the bartender and the doorman about Gus's habit of being at his table every single night. They both backed up the girlfriend's story.

This morning I'd called Luxury Resorts, the timeshare company Ray Candelaria worked for and had been assured that he'd been at work Christmas Eve until six and again on the twenty-sixth at eight a.m. Wouldn't have been impossible for him to get to Albuquerque and back, but it seemed pretty unlikely.

So, I was short on ideas at this point. I still didn't give Gus credit for much in the brains department, and it wasn't entirely out of the question that he might have sent one of his "friends" to convince Paula to pay up and the guy might have gotten a little too rough. However, the evidence at the scene didn't quite work with that theory—no damage to the room, no sign of a fight, nothing stolen from the house. I'd run the idea past Ron when I got home, get his take on it, but didn't think it would exactly get the police hot on Gus's tail.

I settled back in my seat for the flight and two hours later had forged my way through the baggage claim in Albuquerque and retrieved my car from the lot.

It was pretty much on my way home, so I stopped at the office before heading toward my own neighborhood. Sally had left for the day and Ron was sitting at his desk, the phone against his ear. I waved hello and went into my own office to see how much mail and how many phone messages I'd missed. I was halfway through them when Ron appeared in my doorway.

"Back already?"

"And without much, I'm afraid." I laid down the phone bill I'd been studying. "Neither of my two suspects seem quite as likely, now that I've talked to them."

Ron pulled a stick of gum from his shirt pocket, unwrapped the foil, and folded the gum twice before stuffing it into his mouth.

"I just don't see Ray Candelaria as a suspect," I told him. "The man appears to be getting on with his life and didn't seem to be harboring ill feelings toward Paula.

"Gus, the drug dealer, on the other hand, might have had reason to come after her. He just doesn't seem to have taken the opportunity. Several people swear he never leaves his usual spot. Maybe we could ask some questions around town, see if there's anybody who might know something about that dark blue car we noticed prowling around before Christmas. Gus could have very well hired somebody to come after her. Or, Catherine said Paula was bragging about some new hunk in her life."

"I ran the plate on the car while you were gone," Ron said. "Johnny Domingo. Twenty-one years old. Got a rap sheet, petty stuff mostly. Started as a kid taking things from convenience stores. Graduated to house burglaries by the time he was fifteen. Supporting a mild drug habit by ripping off TV sets and microwaves."

"Hmm . . . seems a little young to be a boyfriend. All this time we've been looking for a connection to Paula, but maybe it was simply a case of this kid breaking in, thinking no one was ome. Hoped to score a nice appliance of some kind and get

out. Paula was there and he grabbed the first available weapon."

"With all the traffic in the neighborhood?" He knew a fair

number of people would drive around Christmas night rather

than take on the huge crowds Christmas Eve. His look was

pure skepticism.

"That could be the perfect cover. He might have faked a

breakdown and started walking. We were all out walking the

night before, and no one questioned us."

"And he'd haul a TV set right out past the other drivers

and stash it in the trunk of his car?"

"Nothing like that was missing. However, there are plenty

of smaller treasures around. A camera? Jewelry? Come on,

Ron, there are dozens of valuables he could have stashed into a

pocket."

He gave a small nod of concession.

"Do we know where Johnny was Christmas night?"

"Haven't checked that yet," he admitted. "Let me contact

a couple of people I know." The phone rang. "That's gonna be

Leroy. I'll get it in here."

I fiddled with my mail some more, thinking I should

answer a couple of letters but stalling while Ron made the calls. If we could at least send the police looking at Johnny Domingo, it would take some of the heat off Judy. Make their case against her look iffy.

Ron reappeared. "Well, Johnny Domingo wasn't in jail or the hospital, as far as I can tell. As to where he actually *was*, that's gonna take a little longer."

And it could have been a million places.

"I put a couple of guys on it," he said. "They aren't exactly model citizens themselves, but they'll nose around a little."

I didn't especially care, and certainly didn't want to know who these guys were. I was just happy that we'd found a direction to go that was leading away from Judy.

"While you're at it, know any hit men?" I was only half joking.

He wasn't. "Maybe."

"I'm just wondering how we might find out if Gus hired anybody local to go after Paula. And who it might be." I twiddled a pencil in my fingers. "I do think his girlfriend made sense—he wouldn't have anything to gain by killing Paula. But a hired gun might have gone beyond his duty. Done more damage than planned."

"I don't know . . . this line seems pretty sketchy to me. But
can see what there is to learn. Never know."

That's right—you never know, I thought as I gathered jacket
and purse and headed for my car. I was ready for a fresh clothes
and a shower.

Drake and Catherine were out when I got home but the
two dogs greeted me happily enough. Drake had left a note
suggesting dinner at Pedro's, so I shouldn't bother to make
anything at home. Like I would have leaped right to the task
anyway.

It was only three o'clock and his note said they'd be back
from their museum trip about five. I decided to go next door
and see what had happened with the Garfields since I'd been
away.

Wilbur answered the door after I'd rung twice. His
normally pale face was pasty white. His thin, sandy hair lay
plastered to his head in oily strands, and his hands trembled
noticeably. His pants and shirt looked like he'd slept in them,
and his navy cardigan hung lopsided from his shoulders. His
wire-rimmed glasses had fingerprint smudges on the lenses. He

greeted me with a grunt and stepped aside so I could enter.

The living room showed the lack of a woman's touch. Newspapers and unopened mail were strewn over the sofa and tables. Two beer cans stood on the end table next to his recliner and a dinner plate on the coffee table had something tomatoey dried on it.

"Judy hasn't been released, I gather."

"No. The judge was taking a long holiday weekend and her lawyer hasn't pushed to be assigned to a different one. Her bail hearing is now set for Monday."

"Oh, no. I can't believe that! She shouldn't be stuck downtown just because it's a holiday week. Want me to see if Ron can pull any strings? Call somebody, or get her a different lawyer?"

He didn't seem to know what he wanted. He shuffled over to his recliner and flopped down. I followed and sat on the sofa across from him.

"Ron and I are trying to follow the drug connection," I said. "I met the guy in Los Angeles Paula was buying from. But there must have also been someone here in Albuquerque. Do you have any ideas? Somebody who called her here at the ouse, or somebody she called?"

He sat lifelessly in the chair.

"I found her address book the other day, but didn't find ny local phone numbers in it. Could there have been another lace she wrote them?"

He picked at a thread on the arm of his chair but didn't espond.

"Wilbur, I'm trying to help get Judy out of jail for good. o avoid the hassle and embarrassment of a trial. Can you meet ne halfway?"

"My wife did not kill my mother," he said, slowly and eliberately. "I know this for a fact. I *don't* know anything about ny drug dealers." His voice had rising shrilly.

"I'm not insinuating that you'd normally know anything bout drugs, Wilbur. I'm just . . ."

The true meaning of his words sunk in and my voice kipped as I figured it out.

He saw it in my face.

"Oh my god. Wilbur . . ."

Chapter 14

He stood up and hovered over me.

"Wilbur? What happened Christmas night?" I slid to the other end of the sofa and stood up. "You and Judy went to the dinner party but she got that headache and went to lie down. What were you doing then?"

I was backing away as I asked the question, but he was quicker. He snatched out at me and grabbed my wrist. Twisting it behind me in a sudden move, he spun me around and moved behind me in a flash. The pain in my arm was unbearable.

"Too many questions, Charlie. You're getting too close and I can't let that happen."

He yanked at my wrist until my knees buckled. "That way," he growled, steering me toward the connecting door to the garage. He kept me gripped with his right hand, opened the door with his left. "Down the steps," he ordered.

I stumbled and thought he might loosen his hold, but I felt my shoulder snap instead. I cried out.

"Stay there!"

I halted on the third step. He bumped into my back and began to pull me to the right, so I was stumbling backward while he headed toward his workbench. He grabbed a plastic tie, the long ones used to bind groups of cords together, and turned back to me.

"Put your other hand back here."

"No! Wilbur, wait. Think what you're doing."

"Now!" He yanked my wrist again. The pain shot through my weakened shoulder and up my neck. I slowly lowered my right hand.

"You never did answer my question," I said, trying to distract him from his work. "What were you doing while Judy was nursing her headache? You came back here, didn't you?"

He was fumbling slightly with the plastic tie, trying to keep a grip on me and operate both ends of it at the same time.

"You made some excuse and came back here, knowing Paula was alone and thinking the police would probably attribute it to a break-in. You knew you could get rid of her."

"I didn't plan it," he whined. "Not like you're saying."

"But you'd had enough of her, hadn't you? She'd never treated you like a man. Never listened to your opinion. And you'd never been able to stand up to her, your whole life, right?"

"I just came back for Judy's migraine medicine. I'd told our hosts I'd run to the convenience store and get something for her, but then I remembered she had this prescription that worked really well. So I came back here."

"And the police never asked your hosts if you'd left the party, did they? They latched onto Judy and went with her as their suspect."

"I never thought that would happen. I *never* meant . . ."

I tried withdrawing my free hand, hoping he wouldn't notice.

"No, Charlie! Don't try it."

"So what happened when you got here, Wilbur? Paula started in on you, didn't she? She was nagging, giving you a hard time, wasn't she?"

"She . . . she said . . ." His voice cracked. "She wanted to stay here and show us how to raise our baby. Said Judy and I were so stupid we'd never be able to do it by ourselves. She'd had some drinks. I just couldn't handle it. The thought of her ruining one more little life. The thought of Judy leaving me— because I knew she'd never go for it."

"And then what? A nice guy like yourself doesn't usually just pick up a fireplace poker because someone insults him."

"She laughed." His face turned grim and I could see him reliving that horrible scene. "She laughed at me and I just snapped."

"Wilbur, let me go. I'm sure there's a way we could explain this to the police."

"Hunh-uh. They might let Judy go but then our baby's father would be in jail. I can't have that. You're the only person who's come close to figuring it out, Charlie. I just have to think what to do with you. I already have a plan for getting Judy out."

"Wilbur, think about this. If you get rid of me, you'll have two mur—"

"Shut up! I mean it!"

Quick as a flash, he grabbed my free hand and was about to snap the plastic clip on me. It was now or never. I stomped on his instep as hard as I could and followed immediately by flinging my right arm toward his face. I clipped him across the ear but it was enough to make him drop his grip on my pulsing left wrist. I spun to face him, scanning the workbench behind him for a weapon, any weapon.

He'd had the same thought. He pulled open a drawer at his side and came out with a can of spray paint. I almost chuckled at the vision of myself with a green face, but checked it just in time. Women who laughed at Wilbur didn't last long. All he had to do was temporarily blind me and I'd be bound and gagged and in the back of his car before I knew it. I ducked and ran behind the car.

"Wilbur, slow down. This isn't the way to do this. Getting rid of me will just be the beginning of your troubles."

He held the can above the roof of the car, ready in case I raised up. I watched him through the windows, staying on the opposite side. My mind whirled. I had no idea what time it was, but didn't realistically expect Drake for at least another hour. I couldn't fend off Wilbur that long. I edged my way around the car, coming up on the driver's door. I could always lock myself inside and make him break a window to get at me. Dumb idea, Charlie. He had the keys. If I could just . . .

I edged toward the front bumper. He'd been following my moves, trying to get closer to me. He was now at the rear bumper. I decided to make a run for it before he caught on to what I was doing. I ducked and ran around to the passenger side and up the steps to the house. In a flash I was inside and I snapped the deadbolt behind me.

The front door. I raced to it and locked that deadbolt too.

Wilbur was still pounding on the garage door, but it would probably only be a matter of moments before he figured out that he could hit the electric opener switch and get out. If he had his keyring in his pocket, neither the house, the garage, nor the car would be safe for me. I had to get out of there. I ran to the kitchen door. The pounding at the garage door had stopped.

I grabbed the kitchen phone and dialed 911, laid the receiver on the counter, and screamed as I headed for the back door leading to the yard. I hoped the operator wouldn't talk to the empty phone too long before she sent help to this address. I peeked out the glass panes at the top of the door. No sign of Wilbur.

Then I heard the front door creak open.

Chapter 15

The front door closed with a stealthy click as I fumbled with the locks on the back door. Finally. I yanked it open. A siren screamed through the house as the burglar alarm went off.

Wilbur had obviously set the alarm as soon as he came in, hoping to catch me if I tried to escape. He appeared at the kitchen door as I raced onto the back patio. I headed toward my own house and belatedly remembered that my purse and keys were sitting beside the sofa on the floor in his living room.

"Looking for this?" he taunted from his back door. My purse dangled from his fingers. In his other hand he carried a claw hammer.

Shit.

He sprinted across the patio. I raced away, trying to stay beyond his reach.

Think, Charlie, think. Where could I go? I thought of Elsa's, my safe haven for much of my life, but knew I'd never make it. He'd easily be upon me before she could shuffle to her door to answer my knocks. Besides, I would never put her life in danger too. No, it had to be somewhere else. I headed down the street, opting to leave the relative quiet of our neighborhood for busy Central Avenue. It was six blocks away, but at least there would be traffic and people. Somewhere in the distance a siren wafted lightly on the wind.

Two blocks later, I was beginning to regret my recent lack of exercise. I made a hasty New Years resolution, the same one I'd probably made last year at this time. My legs burned and the air in my lungs felt like fire. Wilbur was keeping a surprisingly good pace for someone who looked like he never did anything more physical than punch buttons on a calculator. He was no more than fifty feet behind me.

Ahead, a cross street bisected my path and I prayed there would be no oncoming traffic because I wasn't going to have the luxury of stopping to take a look. Wilbur was closing quickly. My feet pounded on the sidewalk, my breath rushed in and out with a sound like a charging bull, and somewhere— much nearer than before—the siren entered my consciousness.

The cross street was about thirty feet ahead of me. I made a snap decision. Just before I came to the intersection, I spun to my right and cut across the yard on the corner.

Wilbur's momentum carried him straight toward the street. The oncoming police car, with lights and siren wailing, was only going about thirty. His body smashed into the driver's-side fender and it flung him through the air and into the yard on the opposite corner from where I ran. I caught a glimpse of all this just before I collided with a huge blue spruce tree and found myself stabbed in the face with a thousand needles.

Chapter 16

The mess wasn't nearly as bad as I'd envisioned. My face felt like a pincushion and looked like I had a delicate rash for about a week. Wilbur was lucky, too. His injuries consisted of a concussion and a broken leg, both of which were treated with one night's observation in the hospital before he was released to the custody of the Albuquerque Police Department.

Judy came home as soon as I told the authorities of Wilbur's confession. She looked a whole lot better after a shower and good night's sleep at home. We spent several afternoons talking at my kitchen table. She'd decided to move back to her hometown. It turned out that Wilbur wasn't the only one who suffered intimidation at the hands of an oppressor. While Wilbur had taken his mother's belittling for years, he'd dished out much of the same to Judy. From my own experience, watching his personality go from docile to almost manic in a few moments, I could believe it.

Kent Taylor probably suffered the worst from the whole ordeal. It just about killed him to admit that he'd jumped to much too quick a conclusion about the perp in this case and that he should have conducted a more thorough investigation.

Drake and I are doing great—missing Catherine a little because she really was a good houseguest over the holidays—but happy to have our space back to ourselves.

Here are two free recipes from this story!

Green Chile Stew

1 to 1-1/2 lbs pork tenderloin, cut in 1/2" cubes

2 cans stewed tomatoes, crushed

1 small can mild whole green chiles (4 to 5 chile pods), cut into stew-sized chunks

Hot green chile to your taste (1-2 T. diced)

1 medium onion, cut into stew-sized chunks

2-3 cloves garlic, minced

8-10 c. beef bouillon

Salt and black pepper to taste

2 medium potatoes, peeled and cut into 1/2 inch cubes

Place all ingredients except the potatoes into a large stew pot. Bring to a boil, then cover, reduce heat and simmer 2-3 hours. About 30-45 minutes before you plan to serve, peel and cut the potatoes and add them to the stew. Serve with corn bread, warm flour tortillas or other favorite bread.

Biscochitos (Mexican Christmas cookies)

1/2 c. sugar

1 c. shortening

1/2 t. anise seed

2 c. white flour

1 c. whole wheat flour

1/2 t. salt

1 t. baking powder

1/3 c. water (+ or -)

Cream shortening and sugar together, beating until light and fluffy. Add anise. Sift flours, salt, baking powder together and add to shortening mixture. Add just enough water to hold mixture together. Roll 1/4" thick and cut with cookie cutters. Dip in a mixture of cinnamon and sugar. Bake at 350 for 10-12 min.

Books by Connie Shelton

The Charlie Parker Series
Deadly Gamble
Vacations Can Be Murder
Partnerships Can Be Murder
Small Towns Can Be Murder
Memories Can Be Murder
Honeymoons Can Be Murder
Reunions Can Be Murder
Competition Can Be Murder
Balloons Can Be Murder
Obsessions Can Be Murder
Gossip Can Be Murder
Stardom Can Be Murder
Phantoms Can Be Murder
Buried Secrets Can Be Murder
Legends Can Be Murder

Holidays Can Be Murder - a Christmas novella

The Samantha Sweet Series
Sweet Masterpiece
Sweet's Sweets
Sweet Holidays
Sweet Hearts
Bitter Sweet
Sweets Galore
Sweets, Begorra
Sweet Payback
Sweet Somethings
Sweets Forgotten
The Woodcarver's Secret

Sign up for Connie's free mystery newsletter at
www.connieshelton.com
and receive advance information on new books, along with
a chance at prizes, discounts and other
mystery news!

Contact by email: connie@connieshelton.com
Follow Connie Shelton on Twitter, Pinterest and Facebook